THE UNEXPECTED
WEDDING GUEST

———

AIMEE CARSON

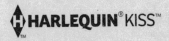

Recycling programs
for this product may
not exist in your area.

ISBN-13: 978-0-373-20720-6

THE UNEXPECTED WEDDING GUEST

Copyright © 2013 by Aimee Carson

HARLEQUIN®
www.Harlequin.com

ABOUT AIMEE CARSON

The summer she turned eleven, Aimee left the children's section of the library and entered an aisle full of Harlequin novels. She promptly pulled out a book, sat on the floor and read the entire story. It has been a love affair that has lasted over thirty years.

Despite a fantastic job working part-time as a physician in the Alaskan Bush (think *Northern Exposure* and *ER,* minus the beautiful mountains and George Clooney), she also enjoys being at home in the gorgeous Black Hills of South Dakota, riding her dirt bike with her three wonderful kids and beyond-patient husband. But, whether at home or at work, every morning is spent creating the stories she loves so much. Her motto? Life is too short to do anything less than what you absolutely love. She counts herself lucky to have two jobs she adores, and incredibly blessed to be a part of Harlequin's family of talented authors.

Other Harlequin® KISS™ titles by Aimee Carson

First Time For Everything

This and other titles by Aimee Carson are available in ebook format. Check out **www.Harlequin.com.**

To my colleagues and friends
at the Yukon Kuskokwim Health Corporation
who, day after day, battle geographical challenges
and unforgiving elements to provide care to the
wonderful people of the Yukon Kuskokwim Delta.

THE UNEXPECTED
WEDDING GUEST

PROLOGUE

———

Ten years ago
Hillbrook University Campus, upstate New York

"I can't believe this is our last night together as roomies," Reese Michaels said as she shifted in her chair on the back porch of the house, feeling restless.

Surrounded by her three roommates, she stared out at Hillbrook College's track field and the rolling hills beyond, countless variations of green lit by the late-afternoon sun. Hyacinths in bold yellows and pinks and purples dotted the yard, the air infused with the clean scent of spring in upstate New York. Everything was new. Changing. As was her life. And not just because the Awesome Foursome, as their neighbors had dubbed them, were going their separate ways.

The gloomy thought was pushed aside as a nervous excitement bubbled up, and she longed to share the news with her friends. The news that she and Mason had secretly spent this morning applying for a marriage license...

"At least we have our road trip to look forward to,"

Marnie drawled, the blonde's every word infused with a hint of the South. "But, Reese, we never would have forgiven you if you hadn't made it back for tonight's last hurrah in the house."

"Though we do understand why you've been so busy with that gorgeous Marine of yours," Gina said with a shrewd smile.

A familiar feeling settled low in Reese's stomach—a funny combination of heat and expectant anticipation that left her heart trying to outdo its previous record. Every time Mason crossed her mind, which was pretty much every 2.5 seconds, that same sensation rolled through her chest. Making her feel happy and hopeful and hungry to hold him again. A smile tugged at the corner of her mouth.

"Look at her," Gina went on, her British accent infused with delight. "She's positively glowing."

Pleased her happiness showed, Reese opened her mouth to blurt out her secret, but Marnie spoke first.

"If you ask me, I think y'all are getting too hot and heavy too fast, honey," Marnie said.

The words pricked Reese's happy bubble, and she snapped her lips shut.

Gina shot Marnie an overly tolerant look. "Most women aren't saving themselves for marriage."

Marnie tucked her hair behind her ear. "There is nothing wrong with saving yourself for marriage."

"I didn't say there was anything *wrong* with it," Gina said before lifting a brow dryly. "But there's plenty that isn't *right*."

With a sigh, Reese listened as they continued the year-old argument. Sweet, Southern, fair-headed Marnie versus cynical, sexy, dark-headed Gina. And then there was plain, practical Cassie, the Australian astronomy student who was too intelligent, too engrossed in trying to discover the secrets of the cosmos to let a mere man occupy any of her time.

Tell them, Reese. Just tell them you're getting married in a few days.

Maybe she should spring the news gently. Ease them into the idea.

Bracing for the response, hoping for the best, Reese tested the waters. "Mason is The One."

Of that she was quite sure.

A stunned silence was followed by a chorus of groans, but she refused to cringe at the naive-sounding statement.

"Oh puh-lease, pass the puke bucket." Gina rolled her eyes in her trademark way. "You're such a hopeless romantic, Reese," she said. "You don't actually believe those chick flicks you like to watch, do you?"

Reese fought to keep her disappointment from showing. Of the three women, Reese had thought Gina, at least, would offer support.

"There's no way you could have fallen in love with him at first sight. Lust definitely," Gina went on. "But not love."

Reese twirled the stem of her empty champagne flute, her voice soft. "But I did."

Ever the sensible one, Cassie, stared at her, her Aussie accent thick. "But how much can you know about each other after only one week?"

With a frustrated frown, Reese tucked her feet under

her legs. She knew it didn't make sense. She knew it was crazy.

But eight days ago she'd settled on the bar stool next to Mason in that mom-and-pop diner in Brooklyn and been instantly transfixed. Not by the chiseled chest and arms, the handsome face, or the brown hair with the adorable cowlick. She blamed the beautiful hazel gaze lit with mischief and cocky arrogance. Radiating confidence. One look and she'd just...known.

Her heart had checked out and there was no hope for a return.

It didn't matter who he was or what he did for a living. It didn't matter that her parents would hate him for...well, *everything*. Daring to be from a run-down neighborhood in New Jersey. Daring to be a lowly grunt in the Marines. And daring to steal the heart of the daughter they'd slotted for the perfect match since infancy, like some ridiculous children's princess movie.

"In a world with billions of people," Cassie went on with a logical tone, "meeting The One is a statistical improbability."

"I have to agree with the supergeek here," Gina said with a tip of her head toward Cassie. "You've met one of The Many, Reese. Mason is a hottie, but you've simply fallen victim to your libido. Still—" Gina smiled, clearly oblivious to Reese's sinking heart "—I say enjoy the shagging while it lasts."

Needing a moment to regroup, hoping to figure out how to share her news, Reese stood and picked up the empty champagne bottle. "You have sex on the brain, Gina," she said as she headed for the kitchen.

"Exactly," Gina called after her. "So when you come back, we want *details*."

Heat flushed up Reese's face as the back door closed behind her, because the details would be juicy indeed. She certainly was enjoying every moment she spent in Mason's bed, but their relationship was so much more than physical. Because Mason had changed her for the better.

Her nineteenth-century history professor didn't intimidate her anymore, her mother's overbearing phone calls were easier to endure and her future felt bright, instead of daunting.

Reese pulled a bottle of champagne from the stainless steel refrigerator and tossed a popcorn bag into the microwave, turning it on. As the popping sounds slowly increased in frequency, she chewed on her lower lip, remembering their scoffing reaction to her claim that Mason was The One.

Their insistence she was blinded by great sex.

So, okay, maybe it had been difficult leaving Mason's bed early this morning for the long commute back to Hillbrook. Especially after he'd sneaked up behind her, slipping those muscular arms around her hips. As soon as he'd pulled her against that well-honed, boot-camp trained body, she'd been a goner. The tiny kitchen in his New Jersey hole-in-the-wall apartment barely contained room enough to think. But Reese didn't care, because it was *Mason's*. He'd slid those calloused fingers around her waist, one hard hand heading north, and the other south....

Instantly compliant, she'd arched her back and given herself over to his plans, her history final the furthest thing from her mind. The fiercely intense way he took her left her both shattered and reborn. Every single time. And so high on life, on *love,* if she sold the emotion on the steps of the UN building, world peace would be all but secured. So when Mason had asked her to marry him, she'd said yes.

Marrying Mason would be the easy part.

Telling her family and friends would be hard.

The scent of scorched popcorn brought her back to the present, and she rescued the bag, dumping the contents into a bowl. One arm around the container, she grabbed the champagne and headed out the back door. As she stepped out onto the deck overlooking the beautiful yard, the men's track team now gathering on the field beyond, she caught the end of Marnie's statement.

"It's going to be a gorgeous wedding," the blonde drawled.

Reese's heart stumbled. "Whose wedding?" she said as she crossed back to the three women.

Gina's British accent was heavily marked with sarcasm. "Marnie's big brother, Carter, to that sweet little Southern cookie of his." She rescued the bottle from Reese's arm, as if desperate for a drink. "What took you so long?" Gina said with a faint scowl. "And how can people be so stupid as to get married at our age?"

Reese blinked, stunned into silence.

Cassie, her eyes far too intelligent and serious, wrinkled her nose. "You burned the popcorn."

Or maybe the scorched scent was coming from Reese's brain as she furiously scrambled for another approach to share her plans. Because how was she supposed to deliver her news now that Gina had declared the idea of marriage at their age ridiculous? Gina opened the champagne and refilled their glasses as Reese collapsed onto the chair, setting the bowl on the table surrounded by her friends.

"So many gorgeous men," Gina said, eyes on the male runners preparing for practice. A collection of long, lean legs stretched...muscles and sinew rippling, tanned skin gleaming in the late-afternoon sun. "So many reasons to shag them and then forget about them."

Which, even coming from Gina was a bit too much.

Reese narrowed her eyes at Gina. "What has gotten into you tonight?"

"Nothing." Gina slumped deeper into her chair.

"Admit it, Gina," Marnie said to the brunette. "The reason you chose to room with us is because Reese's house has a front row view of the athletic field."

"Too right. I love our nightly bitch sessions on the porch." Gina popped a kernel into her mouth, making a face. "Charred popcorn and Dom Pérignon," she said. "I can't wait to see what kind of wedding you'll throw one day, Reese."

Reese's heart twisted tight. Did a stand up quickie in front of the justice of the peace count? Probably not.

But Gina, lovely cynical Gina, only made it worse when she said, "And since you're the only Park Avenue Princess among us—and I for one *never* plan to tie myself to just one man—I'm going to have to get my wedding fix through you. So it'd better be fab."

Reese coughed on her champagne. "The ceremony isn't important, only the man. I'll be happy with a simple wedding."

The disbelieving laughs from her friends weren't encouraging. Did they really think she was so shallow?

"Please. Most students live in a dorm or an apartment.

Your parents bought a beautiful house for you on campus," Gina said.

"And provided a maid service," Cassie said.

"Exactly," Gina said. "So you know they'll throw a wedding that will outdo the Royal Family."

"Honey, you might be obsessed with Mason *now*," Marnie added, her Southern roots drawing out the last word. "But you know you'll marry some high-powered Wall Street figure your Mom and Dad approve—"

"No," Reese said, so firmly the three women looked at her in surprise.

She waited a moment before going on, hoping to emphasize her point. The point being that her upbringing was irrelevant, *despite* what her friends said.

"When I say I do, it will be for love." Reese forced herself to rein in the intensity of her voice. "And it will be forever," she said, fingering the dog tags hidden beneath her blouse.

Mason had placed them around her neck this morning, telling her to think of him until they met up again at the city clerk's office. And the plain chain that bore the metal with Mason's name was more precious to her than any five-carat diamond engagement ring. Or even the Tiffany emerald necklace her parents had given her on her birthday.

Her *parents*.

Reese's fingers clamped around the dog tags. "When I get married," she went on, "money and status won't be a consideration."

Gina hiked a skeptical brow. "Have you told your mom and dad this?"

"I'm nineteen years old," Reese said, abandoning her

plans of sharing her secret. "I don't need permission to marry." Pushing aside her worries, she raised her glass and changed the subject again. "To our last night as roomies."

Faces instantly gloomy, they lifted their drinks in response, and affection pinched her chest.

"You know I love you guys, right?" Reese met their gazes. She knew they'd forgive her for keeping her secret until she was officially Mrs. Mason Hicks. "So this isn't the end of the Awesome Foursome," she said, too full of hope not to smile. "This is just the beginning."

ONE

———

Reese stood on the small platform in the elegant sitting room furnished in eighteenth-century antiques, smoothing her hands down the satin. The wedding gown fit her waist just right, hugging her body to her hips before flaring in a dreamy swirl of tulle that floated to the floor, one hundred yards total. She had only one issue with the dress, and, unfortunately, the problem was getting bigger. Or technically, smaller. With a frown, she reached into her strapless bodice and adjusted her right breast.

"Don't bother." Amber met her gaze in the full-length mirror, her words muffled by the pins in her mouth, her hands fingering the bodice at the seam. "We need cream puffs."

With a sigh, Reese dropped her hand to her side, staring at her reflection. Proof positive that God was indeed male. Because there could be no justice in a world that declared a woman must lose weight in her boobs first.

"Is that the best my seamstress, bridesmaid and future sister-in-law can come up with?" She sent Amber a dry look. "Your breasts are shrinking so bring on the cream puffs?"

The redhead's face flushed with pleasure. "Your brother and I aren't engaged."

"Yet," Reese said with a smile.

Amber removed the pins from her mouth. "We're here to talk about your wedding," she said. "And at this rate, you won't have anything left to fill out your dress. Do you *want* the bodice looking like the empty bucket of a bulldozer as you make your way up the aisle?"

Her friend stabbed a pin through the fabric under Reese's left arm before she went on. "I told you to stop stressing about the wedding and let the event planner do her thing."

"She's driving me crazy."

"You hired her to do a job," Amber said as she continued to work, her voice firm. "So let her do it."

"But she keeps forgetting it's *my* wedding," Reese said. "Why else would she act as if she has such a vested interest in the bride and groom's first dance?" She blew out a breath. "I swear I spend more time defending my choices to her than anything else."

Amber shot her a concerned look. "Keep this frantic pace up and I'll be altering this dress the day of your wedding. Which, I might add—" she jabbed the last pin into place "—is only six days away."

The knot of anticipation tightened in Reese's belly. Six days to ensure every detail was just right. But as she stared out of the second-floor window at the manicured grounds of Bellington Estate—grounds that included several formal gardens—a sense of peace rolled through her body. June in the Hamptons was gorgeous. Spring showers had done beautiful things to the one hundred acres that surrounded the twenty-five-bedroom, historical home, the closest thing to a castle that Reese could find.

The perfect place for her fairy-tale wedding.

But it wasn't the antique-adorned rooms, the priceless artwork, or the towering stone turrets that had sold her on the location. Yes, the grounds were perfect for an outdoor wedding reception. Yes, the restaurant-quality kitchen had a walk-in freezer capable of housing as many ice carvings as she wanted, personally inspected and approved by the sculptor located half a state away. But what convinced her to book the wedding here was the stately feel, the sense of serenity that Bellington Estate brought. It had been worth the two-year engagement to Dylan.

The right location for the right wedding to the *right* man.

Satisfaction swelled, and she let out a contented breath. It certainly beat an impulsive ceremony in a county courthouse. The swirl of roller-coaster, nauseating excitement. And a cocky Mason in his military fatigues, his feet shifting impatiently as they stood before the judge. Reese in her simple sundress...

Anger and hurt rose up, as familiar as her own reflection, and she pressed her lips flat, shoving the ten-year-old memory aside. That was then, and this was now. Dylan made her happy. He made her laugh. They were a great team, not only professionally in her position as chairman of fundraising for The Brookes Foundation, his family's charitable organization, but personally, as well. They rocked the compatibility charts in every way.

Dylan deserved a beautiful wedding. After all these years, *she* deserved one.

Reese glanced back at her bodice and tried to shift her left breast higher, hoping to fill the gap.

"Rearranging them isn't going to help. The girls are looking a little malnourished."

The male voice slid through her consciousness, triggering long-suppressed emotions that came bubbling up like an ominous ooze. Her heart set up house in her throat, making speech impossible, and Reese slowly removed her hand from her bodice. Shifting her gaze in the mirror, she took in the lean, muscular form lazing against the doorjamb. The familiar potent power and arrogance were not lost in the reflection as, arms crossed, Mason Hicks met her eyes in the mirror.

Reese blinked, hoping the figure staring back at her was a trick of her imagination, the voice emanating from inside her head. Visual and auditory hallucinations would be most welcome in comparison. There were treatments for those, but all the medication in the world couldn't see her through a visit from Mason. And the intensely curious look on Amber's face was proof positive that her ex-husband was indeed...*here*.

"Girls?" Reese repeated, feeling stupid.

"Puppies," he said. His thickly fringed, hazel eyes were lit with mischief as he crossed the room in her direction. And every footstep ratcheted her heart rate higher. "Bazookas."

His disturbing gaze grew closer, and, just like when they first met, elicited the same burning low in her gut. His chest looked as cut as ever beneath his military, olive green T-shirt. And pretty soon he was standing next to her, near enough to smell his musky, masculine scent. Close enough to touch.

And her expression must have remained as blank as her brain.

"Boobs," he clarified.

The word finally shattered the trance, the same sensual web the man had magically spun so many years ago. But she was older now.

Wiser.

She narrowed her eyes at him, daring him to continue with his man-thesaurus listing of names for the female anatomy. Instead, he took the direct approach.

"Last time I saw you, your breasts were bigger," he said. "I think a few cream puffs are definitely in order."

"See, the man agrees with me," Amber said, eyeing Mason with interest. "At least have a little ice cream, Reese."

Mason's lips tipped up at one corner. "She loves crème brûlée."

"Topped with caramel topping," Amber added, returning the smile.

Mason turned his attention back to Reese, and looked at her as if she was incapable of intelligent speech. No need to wonder why.

"Surprised to see me, Park Avenue?" The familiar, sexy rumble and the nickname added to the surreal nature of being transported back in time when she had laughingly told Mason her college roommates' nickname for her, Park Avenue Princess. And then he'd made the name his own, dropping the princess part. Which for some strange reason had pleased her to no end.

But she was not pleased to see Mason.

Days away from her *wedding*.

Reese gritted her teeth, struggling to retain her cool as the anger finally built high enough to surpass every other emotion—shock, doubt and dread, just to name a few. Why was he coming to see her again? After ten years, why *now*? Right when all of her dreams were finally about to come true.

And since her appetite had been suffering from the stress of the planning, her chest shrinking, it only seemed fair his muscles should have gone soft, as well. Less sharply defined. Less capable of reaching out to the very core of what attracted a woman to a man.

Strength. Power. And a raw masculinity.

She forced her voice to remain smooth. "And the last time I saw you, you were dodging the dog tags I hurled at you."

"Your aim was good."

Quirking her lips dryly, she said, "I should have used your baseball bat."

"It still made a nice punctuation mark for your demand for a divorce." The corners of his eyes crinkled. "Claimed irreconcilable differences, if I remember right."

She tipped her chin higher. "Temporary insanity was more like it."

"A *lust*-induced state of insanity." Heat flushed through her like a flash fire, though he steadily held her gaze. His expression more reflective than affected, he murmured, "A drug, that."

Her chest pinched, making breathing more difficult. Bad enough he had to still look good, now the unwanted memories invaded. Memories of Mason making love to her. The incredibly intense state of happiness they'd achieved, right before it had all been blown to hell. Correction, right before *Mason* had blown it all to hell.

Remember, Reese. Never again.

Never *again.*

"The sex wasn't a drug," she said, though, at the time, she'd thought the same thing. But God knows she'd learned her lesson the hard way. She was no longer susceptible to the whims of her hormones. "It was quicksand."

And just as deadly to her peace of mind. Her sanity.

He hiked a brow and studied her a moment more. "Maybe," he said softly, his lips curling at the edges. "But what a way to go."

The grandfather clock in the corner ticked loudly, but not nearly as loud as Reese's thumping heart. She smoothed a damp palm down her dress, and shifted her gaze back to Amber, who was looking incredibly entertained. "Can you give us a minute?"

"Of course. I'm done here anyway," Amber said. "I'm supposed to head back to the city to meet Parker for lunch."

"Then go," Reese said. "I'll ask Ethel to help me out of the dress."

She certainly wasn't going to ask her ex to unbutton her gown.

The redhead's eyes lingered curiously as she passed by Mason, but Reese couldn't blame her. Mason exuded a barely restrained energy that underscored the kind of training that meant, when bad things happened, this was the guy who could take care of the problem. But as a husband, he was guaranteed to let you down.

Bracing herself, she turned to face her ex. "I'm sure you're not here to discuss my bra size."

"Nope," he said. "Though I do find the topic fascinating. What are you now?" He hooked a finger in her bodice, just to the left of her breast—the touch sending a sensual shock that left her briefly paralyzed—testing the fit. "B cup?"

She refused to let him see how he affected her. "It's none of your business."

"You're absolutely right," he said easily.

Their gazes locked, seconds ticked by in which she felt overwhelmed, over her head. Drowning in Mason's presence. Just like she had as a young university student. All from the smoldering hazel eyes and the simple masculine finger barely brushing against her skin. And he wasn't even touching anything *vital*.

Quicksand. He's quicksand, Reese.

And for some ridiculous reason she had the intense urge to explain, which made her even angrier.

"You met me while I was a stupid college kid," she said. "A naive junior who was still lugging around her freshman weight and her romantic ideals."

Turns out the romantic ideals had been easy to lose, dropped like a stone during her year of marriage.

The disturbing finger finally pulled away, and Reese's taut muscles relaxed a fraction. Until Mason dropped his hand to the satin at her waist, as if testing its size. "Those extra pounds looked good on you."

Heart tapping loudly, she stared at him and schooled her features into an expression of nonchalance. She would not let him know how disturbed she was by his presence.

"I liked your hourglass figure." His hazel eyes skimmed

her body. There was no lurid component to the look, just a note of concern. "Now you look more like a half-hour-glass."

Reese fisted her hand, refusing to take the bait. He was trying to get a reaction from her. But she would not play into his plans.

His brow crinkled in doubt as he fingered the netting at her thighs. "And the dress is a bit much, don't you think?"

The intricate beading on the bodice was beautiful, though the tulle skirt *was* fuller than she'd intended, floating around her legs like an ethereal dream. But the gown made her feel beautiful. Made her feel special. Just like Dylan did.

In the end, Mason had made her feel like dirt.

"In light of what you wore to our wedding..." He rubbed the netting between his fingers and frowned, and there was a thoughtful curiosity to his expression. "I wonder if maybe you're overcompensating."

Anger surged, and she brushed his hand away, ignoring the sparks that arced up her arm. Her body was simply reacting to the memories. They had nothing to do with the man himself.

Reese turned to face him, braced for the battle ahead. "Trust me, Mason," she said firmly. "Our disastrous marriage was *not* on my mind when I chose this dress." Bad enough she had a wedding planner that questioned her every decision—now she had to defend her choices to her ex-husband? "You need to leave now."

"But I just got here."

"Well, I have a wedding coming up. And I don't have time for your pathology."

His eyes creased with shocked surprise. "Pathology?"

Holding his gaze, she refused to back down as the silence lengthened around them. He knew well and good what she was referring to. When he'd finally returned from Afghanistan all those years ago, they'd tap-danced around the issues long enough to fill two seasons of *Dancing with the Stars*. Reese, gently trying to help.

Mason, coldly pushing her away.

Her ex finally broke their staring contest and headed in the direction of the door, and her heart soared, hoping he was leaving because of her insult. Instead, he turned and sank into a Louis XV-style, wingback chair. And her hopes sank along with him. He stretched out long legs encased in well-worn jeans that emphasized his raw power, and crossed his ankles. The lazy posture was all an act. Because beneath the laissez-faire attitude was a definite edge, as if he was always scanning his surroundings, taking in every detail. Looking for danger. Prepared to react.

Except, of course, when it came to relationships.

"Pathology," he repeated, now looking amused by her choice of words.

Irritation swelled. Wasn't it just like the man to treat the serious issues so cavalierly?

"Surely you didn't come all this way to give me a running commentary on my dress," she said.

"True."

Irritation swelled when he didn't elaborate. "Or comment on my figure."

"Right again."

"So—" seeking comfort, she smoothed a lock of hair behind her shoulder "—why *are* you here?"

And, even more importantly, how was she going to get the stubborn man to leave?

TWO

—

Why are you here?

It was a helluva question.

Should he be flippant and say he wanted to drive her crazy? Because she'd always been sexiest when riled? After ten years she still looked so beautiful that the first sight had been like a blast to his chest—surprising, since his lack of a sex drive lately had started to scare the heck out of him.

Or should he go with the blunt truth: because his shrink had sent him?

Pathology, indeed. A soft grunt escaped, and his lips twisted wryly. As if his screwed-up head could somehow be treated by facing the "unresolved issues in his past." Mason had scoffed out loud at the psychiatrist's words.

Personally, Mason was pretty damn sure his "issues"— the relentless insomnia, the crippling migraines and a sex drive that had gone AWOL—were all the result of the IED that had exploded eight months ago, nearly killing him. Traumatic Brain Injury was the diagnosis, leaving him with a crappy short-term memory, as well. But what difference did a name make when sixteen sticks of C4 had knocked him on his ass on a pothole-filled road in Afghanistan? Where he had lain, unconscious, for two hours before his buddies could extract him from the concrete-littered street.

Why he was still alive, he had no idea.

But essentially, he was here today because he'd more or less been ordered to come. He'd tried everything else, and the medical doctor's only words of encouragement now were that things should get better with time. The operative word being *should*. And then his shrink had insisted that Mason reach out to all the people he'd pushed out of his life over the years, which had been easier said than done. Because, *seriously*, finding closure after his disastrous FUBAR of a marriage with Reese?

Impossible.

But life was difficult while dealing with searing headaches that struck without mercy. If there was any chance at all, no matter how small, that Mason could get closer to his fully functional, pain-free life, he'd grab it with both hands.

Even if he did believe the mission to be a complete waste of time.

He rubbed the scar at his temple, easing the tensed muscles. "Maybe I'm just here to wish my ex well before her big day," he said, knowing she wouldn't believe him.

Hell, *he* didn't believe him.

Reese stared back with those inscrutable blue eyes that, at one time, had been his whole world. But that felt like a thousand years ago. And he'd been a different man. Whole.

Pathology-free.

The irony brought a smile to his mouth as he studied

Reese. Her sleek blond hair gently curled at ends that lay just beyond her shoulders. The style was shorter than when they'd first met, her long hair then a remnant of her youthful years. A girl hovering at the edges of womanhood. Bright. Beautiful. And hopelessly optimistic. And unlike every other female he'd known before or since, completely classy. She had radiated an elegance that had bedazzled the guy from the run-down suburb in New Jersey. Fortunately, his long-term memories were vividly intact, his fondest ones consisting of teaching Reese the joys of down-and-dirty, sweaty sex.

She'd enjoyed every minute of it, too.

He had yet to experience that kind of intensity with anyone other than Reese—couldn't work up an appetite for *anything* since the explosion eight months ago. And while the memories were a reminder of his currently missing libido, unfortunately the shared enjoyment of each other's body had failed to bridge the monumental gap between them. It had simply blinded them both to the brutal reality.

"Not that I think you're telling the truth—" Reese hooked a hand on a hip "—but consider your well wishes received."

"My wedding gift is in the truck."

She looked as if she wasn't sure if he was kidding or not, and then drew herself up to her full height, all five foot four inches of her.

Reese jerked her head toward the door. "You should leave now."

He could, but he was taking a moment to enjoy the view.

The fair features. The wide eyes, so blue they reminded

him of a cloudless summer sky. The full, pink-tinted lips
that had loved every inch of his body.

His voice dropped an octave. "In a hurry to get rid of
me, Park Avenue?"

A small furrow creased her brow. "I'm too old for nick-
names anymore."

"Not true," he said. "We just need to adjust the name."
He nodded at the dress that was fit for a royal wedding,
her legs surrounded by a frothy amount of netting. Perfect. Because she was a foamy, girlie latte whose upbringing had left her too delicate to withstand his bitter, black
coffee self. "I say drop the Park Avenue and just leave it
at Princess."

Was it his imagination, or did her nostrils just flare
in anger?

"My fiancé Dylan is due to arrive any minute," she
said crisply.

"Dylan, huh?" he repeated out of habit.

He pulled out the small notebook in his pocket and
scribbled the name down, in the off chance he needed to
remember. Reese eyed his movements as if he was mocking her by his actions.

If only.

"And I don't think you should be here when he arrives,"
she said.

Unconcerned, he lifted a brow. "Is he going to kick
my ass?"

"Unfortunately, no," she said with a meaningful look.
"He's way too classy for such a juvenile response."

Mason bit back the smile at the indirect insult, tucking the notebook back in his pocket.

No doubt Dylan was the sort of man Reese should have

married a long time ago. Successful. Rich. And from the right kind of family. The kind of man her parents would happily include as a member of the family. Certainly not an enlisted Marine.

But damn it, after eighteen hours of driving—and a migraine that had laid him up in a hotel for another twelve, puking his guts out and so dizzy he couldn't stand—he was motivated, and refused to leave without trying for some sort of understanding. He'd been sent on a mission, and he was going to complete it to the best of his ability.

"We broke things off fairly abruptly." He cleared his throat, shifting in his seat as he went on. For some strange reason, he couldn't meet her eyes. "Left a lot of things unsaid. Said some things we shouldn't have."

In the pause that followed, he finally returned her gaze.

Her voice was firm. "I meant every word that came from my mouth."

His lips twisted grimly, and he hesitated before trying again. "I was hoping we could get a little..." He barely managed not to roll his eyes at the sissy-sounding word his shrink had used, reminding Mason of a bunch of women on a damn talk show. He finally spit the word out. "Closure.

"I am *not* discussing the past with you, Mason."

"I just want to resolve some—"

"No."

Her voice, her face, was resolute.

He stared at her a moment more. Although her demeanor was composed, the underlying animosity rolling off his ex-wife was about as subtle as a friggin' sonic boom. She was too refined to yell or scream—or, as she had all those years ago, hurl objects at him. Back then her emotions had brimmed just beneath the surface, a product of her college years, a brief time when she'd been liberated from her family's thumb. Since then she'd been reschooled, retutored and reprocessed, the real Reese buried under a refinement that made an honest discussion impossible. Being married to her had been downright difficult. But now she was more unapproachable than ever before.

His original assessment was correct; coming had been a wasted effort.

Because one look at Reese's very beautiful, very angry face, and he knew there'd be no resolving any "lingering issues" with the woman. Not only were they too different, too much time had passed. Too many wounds had been inflicted. The kind he was sure went too deep to heal.

Just like his freakin' head.

He pinched his eyes closed, remembering the physical therapy, the struggles with his memory and the resignation that he would never be the same.

Mason heaved out a breath and pushed up from the chair. "Then I won't take up any more of your time," he said, his gaze lingering a moment on the woman he'd once thought he could do forever with.

Her hair, the color of sunshine. The clear, creamy skin of her shoulders. The thinner figure that still held enough curve to entice a man, encased in a dress that was vastly different from the simple sundress she'd worn at their impulsive wedding. The dress he'd been in such a hurry to get her out of so they could spend as much time in bed as they could before he shipped out. Best just to remember their better moments and let go of the bad.

Even if his ex had chosen to do the opposite.

A ghost of a smile tipped his mouth. "Be happy, Reese." And with that, he headed out of the room.

Wasn't it just like the man? Show up out of the blue and tease her mercilessly. Get her all worked up—on purpose, she was sure—and then wish her well before walking back out the door?

"I can't believe he came," Reese said into her cellular as her emotions continued to reel.

She just couldn't wrap her head around the turn of events. When her phone had rung, she'd been staring at the door Mason had just disappeared through. And she was inordinately grateful to hear her friend's voice.

Gina's British accent sounded over the phone. "Who came?"

"Mason."

"The ex?"

Still wearing her wedding dress, Reese braced her hand against the window and stared down at the estate driveway, feeling spent. A delivery van was parked out front, a man unloading the champagne Dylan had ordered for the wedding. A familiar, beater red truck with huge tires was parked next to her Mercedes-Benz convertible. Mason still drove the same stupid vehicle. The Beast, she'd called it. The truck had been old when she'd met him, and now it was positively ancient. The first place Mason had ever made love to her.

She pressed her lids closed, hating how weak she'd been back then.

"Why did he come?" Gina asked.

"He wanted to talk."

"Talk?" Gina said. "I thought you two despised each other?"

Chaos churned in Reese's head, as she remembered the way he'd made her feel at the end of their marriage. Alone. Shut out. Unimportant.

And the man hadn't changed one bit.

Reese fisted her hand against the window. "We *do*."

Though it was hard to separate the hate from the pain.

After he'd arrived back from his first tour in Afghanistan, all the hope she'd felt the day she'd married him slowly seeped away. She'd tried to prepare herself, reading about all the issues of returning to civilian life, PTSD, depression, just to name a few. Hoping to get a jump on the problems to come. But no matter how hard she'd tried, or how understanding she'd been, the old Mason was nowhere to be found. The Mason who'd returned was cold. Unreachable.

Dark.

But most importantly, he hadn't seemed to care, refusing to attend therapy with her. He'd had access to the best care money could buy, but he'd refused to meet her even a quarter of the way. She knew she'd probably pushed him too hard, but she'd missed his wicked sense of humor, the easy laughter. And *nothing* compared to the anger and hurt when he'd announced he was reenlisting and going back.

Because he'd chosen war-torn deserts and dismantling bombs over his wife.

The remembered fury clamped hard in her heart, and she pressed her forehead to the window, the cool glass soothing her whirling thoughts. Because ten years had given her a little perspective. She'd been unprepared for the change, ill-equipped to adjust from a Mason that had seemed to worship the ground she walked on—in retrospect, an unrealistic reality—to one who completely shut her out. Having him turn his back on her had felt so...so...*alien*.

She was wise enough now to realize part of their problems had been *her* expectations.

"Reese?" Gina's voice sounded concerned. "Reese, are you still there?"

"I'm here."

"Just take a breather and have a Cosmo or something."

Reese heaved out a breath, feeling in need of a drink. "Right after I get out of this dress."

Which, with the millions of buttons down her back, was a feat in itself.

Too bad the rest of the Awesome Foursome had yet to arrive. She needed her bridesmaids by her side. She needed a cathartic bitch session with her girlfriends. Unfortunately, ten years ago their last night as roommates hadn't ended as planned, their friendship ripped apart by a secret that had fractured their group into pieces. And her world had never felt right again.

No matter how hard Reese had tried, she hadn't been able to put the foursome back together again. Her wedding was the first time they all were to be in the same room again. And Reese imagined it was a bit like having divorced parents attending your wedding. How did you keep the peace? How did you keep the old resentments from rearing their bitter heads?

Reese was determined to start her happy life with

Dylan by repairing the rift between the friends. What better way to celebrate a bright future with the man who made her happy?

Unlike her impulsive marriage to Mason. The Wedding Mistake, as she liked to call it. Reese bit her lower lip.

"Forget about the annoying ex, Reese," Gina said.

She puffed out a breath. "Believe me, I have."

"And *don't* let him ruin your wedding."

She pictured Dylan's face and immediately felt calmer. "Nothing is going to ruin our day."

Below, Mason appeared in the driveway, heading for his truck, and Reese let out a sigh, the last bit of tension leaving her body. She'd moved on and refused to look back, and she was grateful he was leaving and taking all the turbulent emotions with him.

Because, by God, she wasn't going to let her ex spoil things, no matter how fit he looked in his jeans.

"How are you feeling?" Gina said.

"Good," Reese said, both in answer to Gina and in response to Mason reaching for the door handle on his truck, preparing to leave. She could get back to focusing on her to-do list. The guests would be arriving in a few days, and she wanted everything to be perfect, which included smoothing the road for a reconciliation between her friends. She swallowed hard, remembering why she'd left a message for Gina to call. "I just need to tell you something before—"

Dylan appeared in the driveway, cutting off Reese's train of thought. As her fiancé headed toward her ex-husband, her heart accelerated.

Reese pressed her hand against the window. "Oh, God."

"What's wrong?"

"Dylan is with Mason out on the driveway."

"Do you think they'll exchange words?" Gina asked.

Mason turned to watch Dylan approach, and she recognized the stance her ex assumed. Squaring his shoulders, feet slightly apart. Tensed, as if preparing for an altercation.

The muscles in Reese's shoulders taut, she said, "Knowing the hotheaded, smart-ass Mason can be—" her eyes darted between the two men "—I wouldn't put it past him to muck with Dylan's normally coolheaded demeanor."

Reese trusted Dylan, but she didn't trust Mason. Frustrated, she tried to focus on their expressions, but they were too far away to read.

"Do you think they'll get into a fistfight?" Gina said.

A *fistfight?*

Of course they wouldn't. Would they?

Reese's knees threatened to buckle. "I don't think so."

Then again, she never in a gazillion years would have thought that, after all this time, Mason would track her down.

"You better go down there, Reese," Gina said. "Make sure your fiancé doesn't wind up with a black eye in his wedding pictures."

Reese pressed her lids closed, searching for strength.

Don't just stand here like you're helpless. Do something, Reese.

Now.

Reese whirled away from the window. "Gina, I've got to go."

"Call me with a report," Gina called out just before Reese punched the disconnect button and tossed the phone onto the couch.

Desperate, Reese reached for the buttons at the back of her dress. If she could just release the top few, she might be able to wriggle out. But her arms burned with pain in her attempt, fingers scrambling. Stretching was useless. Straining didn't work. Grunting from the effort didn't help, either.

After five minutes of concerted effort she finally had to accept that, unless she suddenly acquired the abilities of a contortionist, there was no time to change. Abandoning the plan, Reese rifled through her bags, tossing lingerie and toiletry articles aside. Where were her shoes?

Where were her *shoes*?

Please, please. *Just let them remain reasonably calm until I get there.*

Her hands landed on her Manolo Blahnik satin pumps and relief surged as she slipped them on. She couldn't wear flats and let the dress drag, but maneuvering up the endless hall and down the grand staircase in four-inch heels was going to take time. Time she didn't have.

Because she had to reach them before it was too late.

Mason exited Bellington Hall and crossed the brick driveway leading to his truck, passing a deliveryman wheeling a dolly loaded with boxes of expensive champagne. And, although she was all he needed, the Beast didn't fit in at Bellington any more than Mason did, his truck looking out of place parked next to the stately stone mansion and graceful gardens.

A harsh reminder of the feeling of "otherness" that had marked his marriage and his childhood.

As a military brat who rarely attended the same school twice, and a bit of a loner to boot, he'd been the outsider constantly looking in. Mind-numbingly bland years memorable simply for his monotonous existence—a monochromatic gray where his soul had faded and lapsed into a coma. Ironically, while the military-brat lifestyle left him feeling the odd man out, ultimately his military career had given him the first sense of real belonging—thriving in the tightly knit team environment integral to doing his job.

A job he could no longer perform.

With a resigned acceptance, Mason pushed aside the familiar feeling of loss. So life sucked and then you died, but the mere fact that he *hadn't*—died, that is—was enough of a miracle to put the rest of his mucked-up life into perspective.

Though he was still struggling to apply that attitude to his screwed-up head.

Mason reached his truck and then paused, clutching the door handle. A convertible Jaguar had joined the Mercedes-Benz in the drive, and it wasn't hard to guess who the car belonged to. Apparently the successful fiancé had already arrived. Most likely seeking out his bride-to-be at this very moment.

Definitely time for Mason to leave.

A sense of inevitability settled in his gut. He'd tell the doc he'd done his best to put this ghost to rest. But all he'd managed to achieve was discovering just how time had made his ex more beautiful. And more thoroughly pissed off at him.

A scoff of bitter humor escaped just as a masculine voice called out.

Mason spun on his heel and spied a tall, black-haired man exit the front entrance in athletic shorts and running shoes, clearly about to set off on a jog. Despite the casual attire, the clothes reeked of money. And there was something in the man's eyes and posture that screamed breeding. The fiancé.

What was his name again?

For the nth time since the explosion, Mason cursed the short-term memory that had been knocked and scattered like the proverbial loose screws on the floor, making simple tasks a daily struggle. Amazing how much he'd taken for granted the ability to retrieve information from his brain.

"Can I help you?" the man said as he drew close.

For a brief moment Mason considered lying and claiming to be a delivery guy. There was certainly enough activity going on preparing for the big day that one more truck transporting goods wasn't a stretch. But as his mind scrambled for an item he could have believably delivered, he realized he didn't have a clue what kinds of things would be needed in preparation for a regular wedding, much less one at a location as luxurious as the Bellington Estate.

As Reese's fiancé drew closer, Mason eyed the man warily, trying to recall his name. The guy had a good inch or so on him, but Mason was more muscular. He knew he could take him. He just hoped it wouldn't come to that.

"You must be be..." Drew? David? He refused to look at his notes. "Reese's fiancé."

"Guilty as charged." The man came to a stop in front of him and stuck out his hand. "Dylan."

"Dylan." Hell, maybe this time it'd stick. He returned the shake. "I'm—"

"Mason Hicks," Reese's fiancé said. "Awarded Two Marine Corps Good Conduct Medals, a Humanitarian Service Medal and a Purple Heart." Dylan released his hand. "Just to name a few."

Surprise left Mason briefly speechless as he tipped his head in question. How did he know all that?

Dylan calmly studied him. "When Reese and I started seeing each other I had you investigated."

Normally the news would have put Mason on alert, but there was no hostility in the man's gaze. Nothing overt anyway. But there was a cool wariness, a "why are you here?" question in his eyes that was dressed in such a classy air that Mason didn't feel unwelcome. The elegant manners were impressive. The bride and groom-to-be truly were two of a kind.

They were five-star accommodations while Mason could make do in a dusty hole in the ground, if need be.

"Investigated?" Mason said.

Dylan hooked a hand on his hip. "I wanted to know a little about my predecessor."

"What for?" Mason said.

"So I could better understand the man who made Reese so unhappy all those years ago."

Shifting on his feet, Mason rubbed his chin. His day-old growth was rough, and he hated that he felt scruffy next to the well-groomed fiancé. And the man's steady gaze was making Mason uncomfortable. He didn't fit in here. He didn't *belong* here.

It was well past time for him to climb into The Beast and make tracks.

"I'm taking off now." Mason bit back a grin. "That should definitely make her happy."

Better than the lame engraved picture frame he'd brought as a gift.

"But you just arrived," Dylan said. "There's no need to rush off."

Stunned again, this time the ability to speak took longer to return. Was he serious? Or was he just being polite? Or maybe he wanted him around so he could mess with Mason's mind or something—like it wasn't screwed up enough. But Dylan didn't strike him as the type.

"In case you haven't been informed, time has only *increased* my ability to make my ex unhappy," Mason said dryly, surprised lightning didn't strike him for uttering such a massive understatement.

"I'm not sure that's even possible," Dylan said in agreement.

Mason let out a humorless bark of laughter before going on. "I can only imagine," he said. "I figure the best wedding gift I can give the two of you is my departure. Because Reese was adamant that I leave."

An emotion Mason couldn't interpret flitted across Dylan's face, a slight tightening of the eyes that could have meant anything. "I can imagine she was."

He eyed Mason, as if sizing him up. But not only was there no hostility, Mason didn't sense any resentment, either. Just a wary curiosity from the man who was about to marry his ex-wife. At least his hellacious road trip here hadn't been a total waste. If nothing else, he now knew that Reese wasn't marrying a jerk. But did Dylan love her?

But the bigger question was, why the heck did Mason care?

The silence stretched, leaving Mason uneasy. Edgy. He should leave. Reese was not his concern anymore. What difference did it make how Dylan felt about her? It sure as hell wasn't any of Mason's business.

But no matter how hard he tried to push the past aside, seeing Reese had brought up some disturbing memories. Things he'd thought he'd buried long ago. Clearly he wasn't going to get the resolution he sought. But, at the very least, he wanted to take a better measure of the man she was about to spend the rest of her life with. If he knew she was going to be treated well, then that was enough. He'd be content.

And content was as much as he could hope for these days.

Dylan nodded in the direction of a temporary basketball pole set up at the end of the driveway. "You play?"

"Yeah," Mason said slowly. "Seems an odd thing to have had delivered days before a wedding."

"Reese's cousin, Tuck, is my friend and best man. It's a long story, but he had it set up as a joke," Dylan said, and then looked at him curiously. "You up for a little one-on-one?"

Mason leaned back on his heels and shaded his eyes from the sun, studying Reese's fiancé. Playing basketball with his buddies had saved his sanity during the wearisome downtime in the choking dust of a sweltering Afghanistan desert. And there was nothing like a little friendly competition to take your measure of a man.

Dylan was probably thinking the same thing.

Mason couldn't resist a cocky smile, the universal I'm-gonna-wup-your-ass grin that only a man could understand. "You're on."

THREE

———

The rhythmic thwack...*thwack*...
thwack...that greeted Reese's ears as she burst through
the side entrance onto the brick drive didn't sound like
two men beating the living daylights out of each other.
But her trek across the house had taken her so long that,
by now, the adrenaline surging through her body was
prohibitive to rational thought.

She'd gotten turned around in one of Bellington Hall's
endless corridors and wound up way on the other side
of the massive home. And then she'd had to backtrack.
Losing precious minutes. Her mind conjuring all sorts of
horrendous possibilities, she'd scrambled to make up for
lost time and nearly broken her ankle racing down the
stone staircase in her four-inch heels.

Fifteen minutes had passed since she'd dashed out of
the sitting room. Long enough for two men to kill each
other several times over.

Picturing broken noses and bleeding lips, she lifted her
skirt and picked up the pace, the tulle netting flouncing
around her legs with every hurried step. Heart wedged

in her throat, praying she wouldn't wind up with blood on her dress, she rounded the side of the house and came to a halt.

Because there, both shirtless, bodies damp from exertion, were her ex-husband and her future husband... playing basketball.

Shock stuck her shoes to the pavement, and she stared, motionless, as she watched the two men, their faces set with determination. Sunlight shimmied on chests damp with sweat. Pectorals and biceps lengthened and bulged with exertion as they dribbled, and blocked, and alternately attempted a jump shot. A mesmerizing sight that most women would enjoy. A bubble of hysteria rose, and she almost let out a stunned laugh, fascinated by the disparate displays of masculine beauty.

Wearing nothing but athletic shorts, Dylan was taller, leaner, with muscles that showcased his love for running and swimming. His was an agile grace, all lithe beauty and nimble movements. Whereas Mason, in hip-hugging jeans only, was a touch shorter. More muscular. Raw. Oozing a kind of terrible power that was unsettling, disturbing. And dark. The kind of man that could strike with precision and take an enemy out before he recognized there was a threat.

When he turned, her breath caught, his back sporting a beautifully tattooed pair of angel wings.

After a failed layup, Mason grunted out something she couldn't hear, and Dylan responded with a smile and words she couldn't make out. But Mason's answering bark of laughter echoed across the driveway.

Annoyed, she shifted on her feet and cocked her hip. Here she'd been, practically killing herself while making the journey to break up a potential fight, worried the men would at least be exchanging heated words. And they had the audacity to be having *fun?*

Dylan caught a rebound off the backboard and pivoted, finally catching sight of Reese.

As if the current situation was no big deal, Dylan said, "Hey, bright star."

The nickname had started as a joke. Back in the days after her divorce when all she could do was mope. And when she'd finally thrown herself into her family's favorite charity, The Brookes Foundation's Home for Battered Women, she and Dylan Brookes had wound up serving on the board together—ironically, the very man her parents had slated for marriage to their only daughter. Dedicating herself to the cause had saved her sanity, and then Dylan had gently eased his way into her life. First as a friend who made her smile, and eventually as a lover who also made her laugh.

Until the dark days had grown fewer and farther apart.

The originator of those dark days shot her a curious look. "I thought it was bad luck for the groom to see the bride in her wedding dress," Mason said.

As always, the man elicited a piercing surge of irritation that was impressive. Because it was *his* fault that she was standing here in a torrent of tulle netting.

Steam had to be coming from her ears. "But it doesn't rank anywhere near the catastrophe of an *ex-husband* showing up just days before the ceremony," she said.

"The timing is definitely inconvenient," Dylan said.

At least Mason had the decency to grimace, a rueful look on his face, and Reese shifted uncomfortably. But she refused to apologize or feel guilty.

Because she did not want Mason getting chummy with her fiancé. She did not want Mason hanging around for her dream wedding. She did not want Mason hanging around, *period*.

She brought her thoughts up short and licked her lower lip. "Dylan, what are you doing?"

Mason looked unconcerned, while Dylan looked down at her as if *she* was the one who was behaving oddly.

"I'm playing basketball," he said.

In exasperation, she blew a strand of hair from her eyes. *Men.* Why did they have to be so literal?

"Yes." Her lips felt tight. "With my *ex-husband*."

Two men studied her for a moment, as if waiting for the punch line. And she had the urge to squirm.

"Did he tell you why he was here?" Dylan asked.

Reese avoided Mason's gaze. "He said he wants closure."

"Sounds reasonable to me," Dylan said.

Reasonable?

Wide-eyed with disbelief, she said, "Right now the only kind of closure I want is the kind that comes with a slamming door, preferably with Mason on the *other* side."

Mason let out a chuckle, and she cast him her best lethal look, frustrated by the amused tilt to his lips, the basketball parked under his arm as if he was waiting on Dylan to continue the game. And then there were all those muscles on his naked chest....

Reese frowned and slammed the door on the direction of her thoughts, turning her attention back to the man who usually made her happy.

But Dylan was studying her with a guarded expression that left her wary, the lingering moment filled with spring sunshine, a rose-scented breeze and the buzz of a bumblebee in the garden. Despite the idyllic setting, an ominous feeling began to build.

But nothing prepared her for what Dylan said next. "I think he should stick around."

Even Mason managed to look surprised.

"You've got to be kidding me," Reese said at the same time Mason said, "Come again?"

"I'm not kidding," Dylan said, as if the words made total sense. "You need to hear him out."

She blinked. *Hear him out?* Maybe she hadn't heard him right. Maybe the bazillion yards of tulle netting billowing around her legs created some sort of sound buffer. Absorbing the words around her. Distorting them.

"Why on earth would I want to do that?" she said.

"He's not so bad."

"Thanks," Mason said. "You're not so bad yourself."

She ignored her ex and addressed her fiancé. "And you're basing your assessment of the man on a fifteen-minute game of basketball?" Why did the male species feel fit to judge a person simply based on their ability to toss a ball through a hoop? "I was married to the man for a year, Dylan."

"The man risked his life on a regular basis to help out his fellow Marines," Dylan said, his voice holding a hint of censure. "He's a decorated hero, Reese. He deserves to be heard."

Mason looked away, appearing uncomfortable.

Reese pinched the bridge of her nose and struggled to remain calm. She didn't care what kind of medals he'd earned. She couldn't, *wouldn't*, rehash the unhappiest days of her life. Especially right before the day that was *supposed* to be her happiest.

She dropped her hand to her side, feeling defeated. "I don't have time for this, Dylan."

Dylan swiped a hand through his black hair, leaving the ends spiked. His eyes held a kind of gut-sinking certainty that made her insides twist. "Why the hurry now? It took you *two* years to set a date for our wedding."

Reese sucked in a breath. Was this the reason behind Dylan's behavior? And how many times did she have to explain? She ignored the curious look in Mason's eyes.

"I wanted to be sure," she said, hating how the words sounded like an excuse. "And I didn't ask Mason to show up—"

Dylan took her elbow and led her into the rose garden.

"It's not just his arrival, Reese," Dylan said in a low voice. He came to a stop and released her arm, his gaze flat as he stared off across the rows of rosebushes. "Personally, I think he's the reason you dragged your feet setting a date."

The words were too big to digest.

"Of course he is," she said, trying to remain calm. "Because I didn't want to screw up again. I wanted everything to be perfect—"

"Exactly," he said. "You seemed more fixated on getting the wedding just right than on our future together."

Her mouth fell open, and she tried to formulate a logical response.

"And when you stand up at that altar with me and say I do," Dylan went on, "I want to know that the only thing on your mind is me." He returned his gaze to hers. "I want to be certain that you've put the past behind you."

"Dylan, I—"

"You know I care about you." He stepped closer, taking her hands in his. "That hasn't changed."

The ominous feeling grew bigger. She needed Dylan to be understanding. She needed him to support her in this. Because she wasn't strong enough to fight both men.

"But we have to start our lives with a clean slate," Dylan went on. "And we can't do that until you resolve this thing between the two of you."

"The only thing left between us is hostility."

"A *lot* of hostility." He eyed her with a trace of suspicion. "Too much hostility. Have you ever wondered why?"

"He's my ex-husband," she said incredulously. "According to standard social conventions, I'm *supposed* to hate him."

"Maybe," he said, looking unconvinced. "But I don't want to marry you until I'm sure there isn't something else going on."

Panic swelled. "Are you canceling the wedding?"

His gaze was steady, as if the words didn't light a fuse that exploded in her head. "I'm postponing it."

She stared at him, her lids stretched so wide she was sure they'd crack. In six days two hundred guests were set to watch her walk down the aisle. Two hundred of their closest friends and family. He just couldn't back out now, could he?

But when she opened her mouth to protest, he interrupted.

"The ceremony is just that, Reese. A ceremony. What's important is what comes after," he said. She blinked back the shock, remembering she'd said that very thing to her friends oh so many years ago. "Our life together."

Good God, how could she argue with that without sounding petty and superficial?

But two hundred people...

He lightly squeezed her hands, as if to comfort her. Fat lot of good that did her now.

"You have to go figure out what it is that you want, Reese," Dylan said as if it were the most reasonable statement in the world.

And as he removed his hands from hers, he gently pulled the engagement ring from her finger, closing his palm around the diamond. The sense of finality weighed heavily in her chest.

"And when it's all said and done, if it's me that you choose," he said, "I'll still be here."

This wasn't playing out at all like he'd planned.

One hour after Reese had come barreling around the side of the house in a cloud of flouncing fabric, interrupting the game of one-on-one, Mason sat in his truck, wondering what had just happened. The animosity and the visual daggers Reese had chucked in his direction had been expected. He'd known all along he'd have to endure a lot of anger before getting the chance at having a frank discussion. In the ideal scenario, they would have cleared the air, reached a tenuous understanding, and then shared a drink for old times' sake. And if he'd been *really* lucky, he would've bought her fiancé a drink and wished them both well.

But nowhere within the range of possible outcomes had he envisioned the groom calling off the wedding.

Reese hadn't wanted him around before, so she sure as hell wouldn't be partial toward his company now. So when Dylan had taken off in his Jaguar to head back home to Manhattan, Mason had climbed into The Beast with every intention of driving away. But something kept him from turning the key.

And when a large refrigerated van pulled up behind him in the driveway, the decision was more or less made for him. The deliverymen were adamant the ice sculptures needed to be moved to the freezer ASAP.

Mason hopped down from his truck and told the driver to pull around back. Feeling fairly unenthusiastic about the errand, he then went in search of Reese. He found her sitting on the bottom stair of the massive Bellington Hall foyer.

An angelic vision in white—the picture of class.

Her wedding dress was a white puff of fluffy netting, the color too close to the shade of her face. Her expression was blank, as if all emotion had been drained from her soul and capped. She didn't look up when he entered, and his footsteps echoed across the endless marble floor as he crossed and came to a stop in front of Reese.

He hated the lost look on her face.

And somehow, he didn't think the arrival of the ice sculptures for her wedding was going to cheer her up. In the silence that stretched, he rubbed his temple, the hint of a headache threatening.

Hell, not now. *Not now.*

"Jesus, Reese," he said, his voice gruff. "I didn't mean for this to happen."

She looked up at him with eyes the color of a summertime sky, and his gut twisted with guilt.

"What did you think would happen, Mason?"

"I sure as hell didn't think your fiancé would walk

away." He plowed a hand through his hair. "After you left, I tried to explain. To talk him out of leaving."

"I called him on his cell," she said. Her lips looked as if they were trying to smile, but he thought he saw them tremble once. "But, apparently he's had his doubts about me for a while."

He was sure the tiny furrow marking her brow was just the tip of the emotional iceberg buried beneath her calm demeanor. And, in some ways, he almost preferred the angry Reese.

"I figured I'd find you pacing," he said.

During their many fights, he'd watched her march back and forth enough.

The smile she sent him lacked humor. "I did pace," she said. "But my time was cut short by my Manolo Blahniks."

He frowned in confusion, wondering who the hell Manolo was and why he was shooting blanks. Until, from beneath the torrent of white netting, she stuck out a white satin pump. The height of the heels pushed his brow higher. How anyone walked in the death contraptions was a mystery.

"Nothing cuts your pacing time more effectively than four-inch heels," she said.

He shifted his weight on his feet, uncomfortable as he stared at the woman who looked for all the world like she'd been dumped at the altar. He felt inadequate. This wasn't his scene. This was not where he excelled.

Put him in a hot desert scraping the ground with his knife, painstakingly following a wire to the detonator of an IED, and he was good to go. Toss in a few bullets flying around him, his team by his side, and he knew what to do. He'd thrived in the adrenaline-packed environment.

Especially after sleepwalking through his vacuous adolescent years. But among all the finery and the emotional land mines...he was lost.

And that summed up their doomed marriage.

A status quo SNAFU—situation normal, all fouled up, in the PG rated version, that is.

There was no easing into the announcement. "Your ice sculptures have arrived," he said. "I sent them to the service entrance."

She rose to her feet with a sigh, a cascade of skirting falling to the floor. With a resigned look, she headed across the foyer in the direction of the kitchen, and Mason followed behind. Captivated, he watched her dress bounce gently with every graceful step. The creamy skin stretched across delicate shoulder blades. Her hair swaying, he remembered how he'd fisted his hand in the gold-streaked strands as he'd made love to her.

A sliver of warmth snaked up his spine, and, after eight months of silence, the sharp slice of sexual awareness was a shock to the system. Nice to know his hibernating libido was finally waking up.

He just hoped the reappearance would extend beyond the ex who hated his guts.

Mason cleared his throat, getting back to the matter at hand. "I could just go tell them to send the sculptures back."

They entered the kitchen where Ethel, the head of the household staff, was directing the deliverymen toward the walk-in freezer.

"I had them trucked in from half a state away," Reese said as he followed her into the icy vault, her breath visible in the frigid air. "Besides, it's way too late to get a refund."

"Then donate them to some needy bride and groom," he said.

Reese gently lifted the bag covering a mound resting on a freezer shelf. The base of a sculpture came into view where, in a swirly font worthy of a wedding invitation, the words *Dylan and Reese* were engraved.

His head thumped harder, but he ignored the warning sign as he stared at the inscription.

"I think the odds of finding just the right couple are pretty slim," she said dryly.

He grunted in agreement.

Reese gently lifted the covering higher, revealing a pair of intricately carved swans, the graceful curve of their necks bent for a kiss. The crystalline ice sparkled in the light, each feather crafted in meticulous detail. Clearly no expense had been spared on the wedding of the century. The one he'd sabotaged by his very presence.

Even if she refused to talk about the past, he at least needed to apologize for what had happened in the present.

He followed Reese back out into the kitchen, grappling for the right words. As always, they didn't come. And the ability was worse since his accident. Two burly delivery guys rolled a cart by with two more ice sculptures and disappeared into the freezer.

How many of those useless ice blocks had she ordered?

Lots, apparently. And as they stood, silent, the two men passed by again only to return with another load. The process was repeated several times, Reese's expression remaining alarmingly blank, and Mason's sense of inadequacy swelled. He definitely should go, but he couldn't just leave her here.

Alone.

Dealing with the aftermath of her fiancé's departure.

"You shouldn't be by yourself right now," Mason said gruffly. "You should call your mom. Have her come."

"Absolutely not." A scoff escaped her mouth that was hardly ladylike. "I love her, but her overprotective ways would only make me feel worse."

"Still treating you like a fragile princess, huh?" he said with a wry smile.

During their marriage he'd found nothing funny about the stifling relationship she'd had with her parents. But back then Reese had been oblivious.

She stared out the window overlooking the garden, her gaze distant, unfocused. "My mother has always been a bit...overbearing."

Mason bit back the urge to agree, proud he was able to keep his mouth shut.

"They were constantly worried about me while I was married to you, and positively petrified for me at the end." She smoothed a hand down her cheek. "But I honestly don't know what I would have done without them after our divorce," she went on softly.

She ticked her eyes back to Mason. "It's been Dylan's steady influence that has helped me deal more productively with their smothering behavior. So much so that they now actually view me as a grown-up who's capable of making her own choices." Her eyes crinkled in doubt. "But I suspect my mother's going to freak when she learns Dylan called the wedding off."

Sure his opinions wouldn't go over so well, Mason let

out an evasive "huh" and rubbed his jaw. Family was definitely in order here, but her father was about as cuddly and comforting as a porcupine. But Mason did remember she had a half brother somewhere.

"Parker?" he said.

Damn, he was grateful the long-term memory was intact.

Reese shook her head. "We're getting along better now, but I don't want to bother him with this. He's busy at work and newly smitten with Amber."

"Amber the seamstress?" He hiked his eyebrows, hoping to annoy Reese. "She's pretty."

She drolly rolled her eyes, and Mason suppressed the grin.

"How about one of your college roommates?" he went on. "What did you call yourselves?"

A trace of a smile appeared on her mouth. "Our neighbors dubbed us the Awesome Foursome."

"Right," he went on. "Marnie, Gina and that brainy Aussie chick—"

"Cassie," she said.

"Surely one of them is available."

"They won't be here for another three days or so."

His eyebrows hitched higher. "They're all coming?" he said. "I thought your little girlie gang busted up before we got married."

"Gina and Marnie haven't spoken since, but I've kept in touch with them all." She gave a small shrug. "I was hoping to use my wedding day as a way to bring us back together again."

He stared at the defeated look on her face. He wanted to tell her he was sorry and get the hell out of town. She smelled like crème brûlée, she looked like an angel in white, though his body remembered just how *un*angelic she could be. And all the good memories were beginning to rush their way past the towering wall of bad. The only thing that kept him going was remembering the fury in her face the day she'd hurled his dog tags at his chest. Oh, and the resentment that simmered in her eyes with every glance.

"So what's your plan?" he said.

As Reese watched three more ice carvings roll by, she looked like she needed a hug. Mason shifted on his feet. Feeling like an ass for every one of the twenty seconds of silence before she answered.

"I'm going to give Dylan until tomorrow to change his mind," Reese said. "He offered to contact everybody this afternoon, but I told him I'm giving him twenty-four hours before I call the guests. In case he comes around."

Mason's heart slowed, and he paused.

She turned to look up at him, her blue eyes clear, earnest. "I made him wait for two years for our wedding day. I owe him twenty-four hours of patience at least."

Of course she did. Because Dylan was one helluva guy.

And wasn't that a cold blast to the fragile threads of his awakening libido. But it was just as well. Their time had come and gone. He'd known that when he'd set out to hunt her down.

As he studied her determined face, he felt it with absolute certainty now.

The thudding in his chest worked its way up to his brain and set up residence behind his left eye. Damn, another migraine coming on. Fatigue and nausea descended like a curtain, and his head grew foggy.

The pounding in the base of his skull grew insistent, and the dizziness predictably moved in next. Sweat prickled at the nape of his neck, dotted his upper lip. And Mason couldn't ignore it any longer. He leaned a hand against the center island, hoping he looked casual instead of wobbly.

If he didn't escape to a dark room soon, he was going to end up embarrassing himself by puking on the yards of white fabric swirling around Reese's legs. A feat he was sure wouldn't win him any brownie points.

Bad enough she'd had her wedding canceled, ruining her fit-for-a-princess dress would probably be the last straw.

FOUR

———

Reese lifted the one hundred yards of tulle of her dress so she wouldn't trip as she paced in front of the bedroom she'd assigned Mason. After several hours surrounded by the flouncy skirt, the gown that normally made her feel beautiful was beginning to get on her nerves. Now it felt like a prison. Weighing her down. And, regrettably, after multiple attempts to find help, Mason was the only one left who could undo the buttons on her dress.

Frowning, Reese warily eyed his door as she made another pass, the pacing easier now that she was in bare feet, her toes appreciative of the plush Oriental carpet covering the stone floor. And very grateful to be out of the four-inch heels. She'd be even more grateful to get out of this dress and relax.

But relaxation was difficult with Mason hanging around.

When the last of the ice sculptures had been stored in the freezer, she'd tried again to get Mason to leave, but he'd refused. Frustrated, desperate to get rid of the disturbing man, when she'd insisted she didn't need company—and God knows he was the *last* person she wanted holding her hand—he'd claimed that, after traveling all night, he was too fatigued to drive.

Reese had wondered if he was using excuses to try and get his ridiculous *closure,* but the washed-out look on his face had finally convinced her to agree. He was absolutely silent as she'd reluctantly led him to the bedroom that had been earmarked for Dylan's parents, not even his usual grunt in response to her questions. She'd granted him a *one*-night stay and then escaped, ready for a bath, a drink and her pajamas. As she'd drawn the water in the tub, she'd finally realized her problem.

Which is how she'd ended up here. Outside of Mason's bedroom.

Tulle netting tight in her fingers, she reached the hallway wall and pivoted on her toes to make the return trip, but her voluminous skirt got caught under her foot and she stumbled, almost falling to the carpet.

"This is ridiculous, Reese," she muttered. "Just knock on the stupid door and ask for his help."

Squaring her shoulders, she rapped on the dark wood, preparing for the encounter.

But there was never any preparing for Mason. Because, when the door opened, she was hit with the scent of soap and a vision of her ex, hair damp. He looked as if he wasn't happy to see her, and her throat lost a large percentage of its moisture.

He was in a pair of jeans. And thank God he'd put on a shirt. Because it was bad enough to have Mason undo the buttons on her dress, she couldn't deal with a *barechested* Mason performing the task.

"I need your help," she said.

The only response was an eyebrow that reached for his hairline, and it was then that she noticed his face looked fatigued, faint circles smudged beneath his eyes.

Reese reached up to sweep a strand of hair from her face. "I really want to get undressed." She froze, fingers on her cheek, realizing how the sentence might be interpreted and she hurried to clarify. "I mean, get out of this gown." Unfortunately, her poorly worded clarification wasn't any better. Why did she always sound so stupid around the man? She dropped her hand to her side with a resigned sigh. "Will you please just undo the buttons in the back?"

"What happened to Ethel?" he said.

The caretaker had been the first one Reese had sought out. "I didn't realize she and her husband have the afternoon off," she said. "They went into town."

"Aren't there any other employees around this medieval-sized castle?"

She puffed out a breath, growing weary of the questions. "A gardener who is currently trimming the hedge around the fountain," she said. "Another staff member is up to his elbows in grease repairing an irrigation pump, and I can't find anyone in housekeeping."

The Bellington Estate brochure had promised the staff was discreet, and initially that had sounded like a good thing. Now it was just annoying.

She sent him a pointed look. "And in case you plan on suggesting the men who delivered the ice sculptures," she said dryly, "they've already left."

Despite the fatigue beneath his eyes, a spark of humor lit his gaze. "How long have you been pacing outside of my door?"

She frowned, hating that the man knew her so well. Even after ten years apart.

"Who says I've been pacing?" she said.

His lips twitched, but, fortunately for him, he gave her his typical silent treatment. Which was a wise decision on his part. As days went, today had been one of the worst. And she might just have to hurt him if he called her a liar.

He casually leaned a shoulder against the doorway. "I'll do it," he said. "But it comes at a cost." Her breath snagged in her throat. Loving this man had come at a cost. "I get to hang around until your friends show up."

"Why would you want to?"

"Because your company is so much fun." The sarcastic tone ensured she knew that he was lying. "Look," he went on seriously. "I promise to stay out of your hair. But if you need help...or something..."

Looking awkward, he shifted on his feet.

"I don't need your help, Mason."

"No problem. Then you won't even notice I'm here."

She doubted that, but she chewed on her lower lip, considering her options. Which, from a practical standpoint, were nonexistent.

"Fine," she huffed in resignation.

He stepped back and held open the door. "Come on in."

Reese hesitated again, loath to enter the man's bedroom. But she couldn't very well stand in the hallway for the process.

Just get out of this dress so you can pour yourself a stiff drink before you pour yourself into bed.

With a resigned sigh, she passed through the doorway while deliberately avoiding Mason's gaze, her skirt brushing against his legs as she passed. She was beginning to realize that even if Dylan changed his mind about the wedding, she could no longer walk down the aisle with quite the same spring in her step. Not while wearing this dreaded mountain of fabric.

Feeling awkward, she paused in the middle of the room, taking in Mason's sparse, yet meticulously laid out belongings. Along with the small notebook he'd pulled out during her fitting, his wallet and keys lay on the valet stand, his shoes parked neatly beneath. A pair of jeans lay draped over a hanger. Six T-shirts of the same color, so neatly folded they looked brand-new, sat on the dresser.

Mason closed the door behind her. "I never thought you'd ask me to unbutton you out of an outfit again."

The words tugged hard on her nerves.

"But—I—you," she said as she whirled to face him, stuttering—*stuttering,* for God's sake.

Mason looked as if he'd finally found the amusement in her predicament. She closed her mouth and fisted her hand, refusing to let him get to her.

"And this is definitely the fanciest dress I've ever seen you in," he went on. "Fancier than the one you wore to that Broadway show you dragged me to." His lips crept up at one side. "Though I'm sure this will end differently."

Her pulse skittered, sending sparks to every corner of her body, and the last molecule of moisture disappeared from her mouth.

Although Mason hadn't wanted to visit her mom and dad, much less attend the musical, he certainly hadn't put up a fuss during the limo ride back to her parents' place. Because as soon as the driver had shut the door behind them, Reese had reached for Mason, dragging him to her. Promising to make up for the three hours they'd spent at the show.

It had been a very memorable forty-five-minute trip home.

"Unless—" his brow crumpled in amusement "—you've changed your mi—"

She pressed her lids closed. "Mason, please."

When she opened her eyes again, he was studying her with an expression she couldn't interpret. But he must have heard the tension in her voice, because he abandoned whatever he'd been about to say.

"Well," he said, the glimmer of amusement in his eyes growing brighter, "unless you want me to reach around you from the front—an embrace I'm pretty sure you don't want, you're going to have to turn around."

She blinked, staring at Mason, hating the thought of not being able to see his face. His hands. Not knowing what he was about to do. Not that she thought he was going to try *anything*, but still...

Pajamas, Reese. Remember your new priorities. Pajamas. Drink. Bed. And sleep.

Tomorrow *had* to be a better day. She didn't want to think about the possible ways it could get worse.

She pivoted on her heel, presenting her back to Mason. And, even though she'd braced every muscle, as he swept her hair aside and his fingers brushed against her shoulder blades, a shimmy of nerves unfurled across her skin. Every other sensation faded: the tug on her bodice, the plush carpet beneath her feet, the sight of the antique Victorian bed. Even the feel of the air being sucked into her chest a tad too briskly. She felt little of these things.

Because her entire existence was focused on the tiny

patch at her back where his warm skin grazed against hers. He worked for a minute, wrestling with the top button, and Reese closed her eyes, heat spiraling in her stomach.

Oh, God. I should've just slept in the dress.

"Jesus," he muttered as he continued the battle. "What kind of buttons are these?"

"Mother of pearl," she said, hoping she sounded defensive and not breathless.

The top button finally released. Great. Only twenty or so more to go. Reese dug her nails into her hand, the palm damp. A few more minutes passed, every one of them torture, flames licking along her limbs.

"Haven't you people ever heard of zippers?" he said. "Or were you just trying to drive Dylan nuts on your wedding night?"

She bit her lower lip. "I had a different gown for the reception. This was just for the ceremony."

"No way." His hands briefly paused at her back, and, no matter how hard she tried, she couldn't ignore the heat radiating from his body to hers. She turned her head to meet his gaze, almost amused by the stunned look on his face. "There's enough fabric here to make twenty gowns, and you mean to tell me that there is a *second* dress?" he said.

"A simpler one," she said. "And shoes that would be easier for dancing and an outdoor reception."

He blinked once, and then shook his head, as if she'd lost her mind. She turned to face forward again, hating the way he was dissecting her choices.

"I hope the second one was designed for easier exit," he said.

She had no intention of telling him no.

"The buttons are part of the decoration," Reese said instead.

He resumed his task, and she could smell his musky, masculine scent, feel the warmth of his breath in her hair. Goose bumps pricked at the nape of her neck. As if standing on end to gather additional sensory information. Wanting more, needing to know his every movement.

Most annoying. Because she was having trouble concentrating as it was.

And while he slowly worked his way down, more of his fingers slid between her dress and her back. As he wrestled with a button about halfway down, more of his calloused skin brushed across her, sending a volley of uncomfortable heat coursing throughout her body. No cell was left unaffected.

"Who comes up with such a contraption?" Mason muttered, his voice tight.

"Designers," she said, her voice tighter. "For women who want to feel special on their wedding day."

And remember how unimportant this man made you feel. Remember how lousy he is at relationships.

The process was painfully slow. And with every wrestling session involving a button, Mason's knuckles brushed by, cranking up the nerves and the heat. The sizzling tension gathered like a pending storm in the pit of her stomach.

"I have to ask," he said. "Was this dress your idea?" He paused before going on. "Because it seems a bit much. Even for you."

Even for you. What was that supposed to mean?

"My mother has looked forward to my wedding day since I was first born. And since she missed the first one," she went on, feeling ridiculous for pointing out the obvious, "I figured she deserved to finally have that dream come true."

"Were you trying to make up for not honoring her wish for a fancy wedding...?"

Another button slipped from its loop, and her bodice went a little slacker. Reese pressed her hand to the front, struggling to keep the fabric covering her breasts. Struggling to ignore the feel of Mason's hands on her back. Struggling to breathe.

"Or were you trying to make up for the fact that you married me?" he said.

Her mouth dropped. Palm splayed across her front, she turned to face Mason and tipped her head, finally recovering enough to speak. "I wasn't trying to make up for anything."

And even as she said the words she knew her statement wasn't entirely true.

Worse, Mason stared down at her as if he didn't quite believe her claim, either. And, despite the volumes of fabric and the gapping bodice clasped to her chest, the cool air hitting her back made her feel naked. Exposed. Just like the expression on Mason's face as she waited for his response.

His noncommittal grunt was infuriating, and her irritation rose, despising his go-to nonresponse even more than usual.

"Don't pretend my parents treated you poorly," she said.

"They excelled at tolerating the outsider."

"They treated you like a son-in-law."

His skeptical scowl was intense. "They could barely disguise their happiness when we finally split," he said. "So you're telling me they were thrilled that you'd eloped with a Marine?"

Warmth landed on her neck and fluttered up to her cheeks. "They might not have been thrilled," she said, the understatement almost sticking in her throat. "But they..." She tried again. "They just wanted..."

Her voice died completely as she realized there was no good way to finish the sentence.

"They wanted better for their daughter," he said, filling in where her brain seemed incapable of coming up with an appropriate response.

One that didn't make her parents seem cold.

Reese let out a sigh, giving up. "Mason," she said, "our problems weren't my *parents'* expectations, but ours. We weren't prepared for a real commitment."

She should have known better, because her mother's brief first marriage, the one that had produced her older brother, had ended badly as well. And Parker had suffered as a consequence. Convincing him to participate in the wedding had been difficult, and Reese had finally realized just how poorly her mother had treated her brother. Way back when, Reese had been totally clueless.

As clueless as when she'd met Mason.

"We were simply too young and too stupid to get married," she said.

Mason's thickly fringed, hazel gaze held hers. Convincing him to participate in the wedding had been difficult, and Reese had finally realized just how poorly her mother had treated her brother. Way back when, Reese had been totally clueless. As clueless as when she'd met Mason.

"Too stupid?" His eyes crinkled in humor. "That might be the first thing we've agreed on since I arrived."

Despite her multitude of concerns, the answering smile was difficult to suppress. Because the amused look on his face reminded her of the younger Mason. The one she'd first fallen in love with. The one with the cheekbones sharp enough to cut butter, a full bottom lip that looked hard but felt incredibly soft. The cowlick heightened by the damp tousle of dark hair.

A complete and total hot mess of a man.

The resentment and anger were mammothly dwarfed by the nervous sexual tension that always set her on edge, and several seconds ticked by. Until a quizzical look crossed his eyes as he stepped closer, his gaze forming a question.

Infused with an expectation.

No.

Reese felt the word viscerally all the way to her soul. She didn't want to share a moment of humor. Or a moment of agreement. Or, worse, a moment of…

Heart pounding, hand clutching her bodice to her breasts, she took a self-protective step back. Because, suddenly, she realized all the reminders in the world weren't enough. It might not matter how many times she told herself the man was quicksand.

Not when she was hit with the bleak realization that she was still susceptible to his charms.

And without a word, she turned on her toes and made a beeline for the door.

* * *

The next morning Reese gripped her cellular and struggled to remain calm, which grew more difficult when Mason entered the sitting room, breakfast plate in hand. "The plan makes perfect sense," she said into the phone, picturing her wedding planner's judgmental shake of her head. "I don't understand why you're so resistant, Claire."

God knows Reese had run into the woman's opposing viewpoint often enough the past few months. And why had Dylan's mother suggested Reese hire Claire? Why had the uncooperative woman received such glowing recommendations from her clients? Masochistic tendencies aside, there was zero advantage to paying good money for a smothering dose of disapproval. Her mother provided that and more. For free.

Between Contrary Claire and her ex's persistent presence Reese was going to go berserk.

She was doing her best to ignore said ex, the man wearing his jeans as if he was born to display denim to its devastating advantage.

Who's on the phone, he mouthed.

Wedding planner, she mouthed back.

With a small frown, Mason slid the spinach omelet in front of Reese, surprising her so much that she almost missed Claire's announcement.

"You need to cancel the reception," the wedding planner said.

Reese tried to sound calm. "But I don't want to."

She obviously hadn't done a good job at disguising the

hint of panic in her voice, not if the look that Mason shot her was anything to go by.

As of this morning Dylan hadn't changed his mind, and the thought of disappearing into the mist to lick her wounds was far from appealing. She needed to face the people in her life, head high, and show them that she was okay. Because every time a friend or family member had gotten word of her news, they'd called, and she could hear the concern in their voices. The pity. The worry that poor little Reese was going to break. Parker and Amber had tap-danced around the issue with all the subtlety of a jackhammer.

Her parents hadn't bothered being so discreet.

Claire sniffed disapprovingly on the other end of the phone. "And I'm resistant because I think the idea is gauche."

"You think my idea is—" Reese couldn't believe people still used the word "—gauche?"

Irritation flared, but Reese tamped down the response, vaguely noting that Mason's eyebrows had shot higher as he eyed her curiously.

His forehead bunched as he leaned closer. "Tell her to go to hell," he whispered.

Reese shot him a look as she covered the mouthpiece with her hand.

"Reese," Claire said, as if she were speaking to a child. "I can certainly help you cancel your arrangements."

"Aren't you listening to me?" Reese said to the woman. "I don't want to cancel."

The idea had first come to her while tossing and turning last night, and today, with each call her determination had grown. She needed to show everyone that she could face adversity with courage. That she didn't need their pity. Besides, she'd booked this estate for the week and there was no refunding the money anyway. She'd spent hours choosing the perfect menu, the right decorations.

And she did not want all that effort to go to waste.

What else was she supposed to do with fifteen pounds of caviar?

Reese had friends, relatives and colleagues who had booked a trip to this location. Some were going to stay at the Bellington Resort Hotel in town. Members of the dream-day-that-wasn't wedding party were staying here at the estate. They *all* had plans of enjoying a nice weekend away. And the simple fact that most of them were so sure she'd be falling apart right now made turning the reception into a party all that more important.

She could see the concern in Mason's face, along with a generous dose of confusion. She could only imagine what *he'd* have to say about her plan. Which made Claire's pitying sigh on the other end of the phone more irritating.

But Reese would not let the woman intimidate her.

"This is one of those times when a woman should gracefully exit the stage, Reese," Claire went on.

Reese's jaw dropped a touch. Gracefully exit the stage? She wasn't in some pointless play. This was her *life*. Just where was she supposed to exit *to*?

"I trucked in thirty ice sculptures by the best sculptor in the Northeast," Reese said. "I have enough sautéed scallops stuffed with basil to feed an army."

The confused look on Mason's face broadcast loud and clear that he had no idea what was going on.

Reese pinched the bridge of her nose and addressed Claire. "Are you going to help me or not?"

Mason's eyebrows pulled together and, this time, he didn't bother lowering his voice. "You don't need her," he said. "Just friggin' fire the woman."

Reese closed her eyes. As involved as she'd been in ensuring every detail was attended to, Reese knew that pulling off the party alone would be a monumental task. There was so much to do. So many last-minute details she'd have to handle.

Alone.

"Reese," Claire said. "You need to start thinking rationally—"

Reese had had enough. "Fine," she said, finally doing what she should have done weeks ago. "I'm perfectly capable of finishing this myself."

Reese hit the disconnect button with more force than necessary, driven by the knowledge that she was overstating her ability to pull this off.

She sucked in a breath, steadying her nerves. Her first order of business was to make a list of things to be done. Reese glanced down at her computer spreadsheet and then leaned her head against the back of the couch, her shoulders slumping a touch. The sitting room overlooking the Victorian garden had seemed the perfect place to set up her laptop and start working.

But Mason was staring at her as if he'd arrived at the movie late and had entered the wrong theater, inadvertently winding up in a tragedy instead of the action flick he'd preferred. Her eyes flitted briefly to the window as she desperately tried to ignore Mason's questioning look.

"The staff said you didn't come down for breakfast." He gestured at the plate in front of her and slid it closer. "You need to eat."

Moved by the thoughtful gesture, she murmured a thanks. Mason turned to look out the French door at the gardens beyond, as if uncomfortable with the small amount of kindness he'd just shown his ex-wife. Reese inhaled the smell of the spinach, eggs and spices. Her stomach rumbled, and she realized she hadn't eaten since yesterday at lunch, right before Dylan had driven away with no intention of coming back.

Defeat settled deep. She missed Dylan's easy presence, his relaxed attitude and laid-back smile. In comparison, her gaze darted back to the darkly disturbing man now leaning against the doorjamb leading to the gardens, his hard-cut profile etched in the sun's late-morning rays.

Too bad she'd traded freedom from her dress in exchange for letting him stay.

The olive drab T-shirt was standard military issue and clung to his torso in a way that recalled every detail of his bared chest yesterday, glistening in the sunshine. His snug jeans hugged muscular legs, and a taut backside conjured images of a time gone by.

Mason, naked, striding toward her with that hungry look in his eyes.

Mason, his thighs rock hard beneath her hands.

And Mason...his tantalizing tush shifting as he headed for the shower, leaving her sated in his bed.

Toxin, Reese. Remember the man is a toxin.

And, years ago, she'd indulged in a lethal dose that had nearly done her in.

Fortunately, Mason turned and plunked that distressingly nice backside down on the rose-colored nineteenth-century French settee across from her, and Reese blew out a breath of relief.

"I thought I'd find you calling the guests to tell them the wedding has been called off," Mason said.

She straightened up on the couch. "There's been an adjustment in the plans."

Hazel eyes turned dark, matching the color of his shirt, as Mason looked at her with an expression she couldn't interpret. "Did I sleep through Dylan changing his mind?"

Funny, that. He didn't look like he'd slept much at all. After sleeping for over twelve hours there were faint smudges beneath his eyes, fatigue still etched in his face.

The careful tone in his voice revealed nothing, and she grappled with trying to decide which was worse. The difficulty of having her relationship put on ice just days before her wedding? The humiliating task of dealing with the repercussions? Or the impossibility of doing this all under the unsettling gaze of her too-sexy ex?

"No," she said. "You slept through me telling Dylan I want to turn the reception into a party."

His skeptical hike of an eyebrow said it all.

Well...she didn't need his disapproval. She'd had enough of that from her event planner, thank you very much.

Mason rubbed his chin, as if he had something to say but wasn't going to.

"For a lot of the guests, refunding the airline ticket isn't an option," she said, proud she sounded so logical. Embarrassed she felt defensive. "And since a good number of them were coming in early to go sightseeing, I don't see any reason why they shouldn't proceed with their plans of enjoying their stay at Bellington, complete with a very nice party."

A party that would prove that she was capable of standing on her own two feet.

"Won't that be a little awkward?" Mason asked.

The scoff escaped before she could stop it. Awkward? It was going to be downright difficult. Her annoying wedding planner's opinion had been a shock, but most everyone else had been less than encouraging, as well. Her parents had insisted that the idea was a mistake—her father demanding she cancel and her mother tearfully threatening to drive up from the city just to convince her in person. Even Marnie had thought she was nuts, her drawl growing thick as she'd tried to persuade her to call off her plans.

But Reese wasn't going to change her mind.

Because the one thing she'd learned from her past with Mason was that moping accomplished nothing. Throwing her efforts into the Brookes Charity Foundation had given her a positive goal. And she wasn't going to fade into the background for months on end like the Reese of old.

"Dylan is being very supportive," she said.

She cleared her throat. The statement wasn't a total lie. But the use of the word *very* might have been a stretch.

Still, Mason remained silent, and she shifted on the couch, uncomfortable. She had no way of knowing what the man was thinking. Mason only shared his thoughts when he wanted to, which wasn't often. A fact she'd learned way too late into their marriage. Married for a year, he'd been gone for eleven months of that time. The calls had been infrequent, his emails sporadic. But the communication had been, amazingly enough, *worse* when he'd returned home.

She pressed her lips together and broke her gaze from his face.

"So," she said. "I'm going to spend the next few days removing the wedding from my reception."

"How do you plan on doing that?"

The question was a valid one.

Her determination faltered. "I'm not sure."

He stared at her a moment more, and she cleared her throat, longing to be free of the disturbing gaze. "You don't really need to stick around, Mason. I'm fine," she said as she picked up her plate with the intention of escaping his presence for good.

As a matter of fact, she hoped that was the end of the subject altogether.

"I'm going to help you," he said.

Despite the gut-wrenching *no* her heart spit out, she suppressed the need to utter the word out loud. And the knot of doom—the one that had started the moment she'd laid eyes on Mason—bloomed and grew bigger, pushing Reese's stomach to her toes.

"That's not necessary," she said.

How this man managed to turn her inside out with his mere existence was a mystery. And why was it that the one man she wanted around—Dylan—wouldn't come back? While the one man she needed to leave...*wouldn't?*

She didn't want Mason hanging around in his jeans and T-shirt, those hazel eyes always assessing her, reminding her of the darkness he'd brought to her life.

"You can use the extra set of hands," he said, his expression set. He rubbed his temple, his eyes enigmatic. "It's the least I can do for triggering Dylan's departure."

"Dylan made his choice," she said simply. "You didn't make it for him."

And, for the first time, she realized that the words were absolutely true. As much as she hated having Mason around, no matter how disturbing his presence was, ultimately it was Dylan who had chosen to put their relationship in stasis.

"But still—" he stepped closer, bringing the fresh, musky scent of his shampoo with him "—if I hadn't shown up, you two would be finalizing the ceremony details right now."

"Maybe."

Like a silent movie, her mind raced through all of the feelings she'd had over the past few days. The sensation of something being off with Dylan. The closer they'd come to the Big Day, the more distance he'd sought and the more stressed she'd become. And the less she'd eaten and the more room she'd had in the bodice of her dress.

"Or maybe not," she said softly.

Mason tipped his head, and Reese avoided his gaze. Humiliated she'd been so intent on planning the perfect wedding that she hadn't given enough thought to what was happening in her life.

She knew Dylan had made a valid point about her dragging her feet. Because when he'd first asked her to marry him she'd been petrified of repeating old mistakes. And how ironic that, in an attempt to overcome her blunders from long ago, she'd created a completely new and improved one. Overcompensating for her past had threatened her future.

And hadn't Mason said just as much about her wedding dress?

Mind now swirling, she studied Mason's closely cropped hair, naturally thick and richly textured, emphasizing the cowlick that she'd found so charming. Just like when she'd first met him at the diner, before he'd gotten the buzz cut and been shipped overseas—a look that had made him appear harder, just like the expression in his eyes once he'd returned.

The resulting sharp jab to the heart left her feeling exhausted. Needing escape.

"Regardless of the reasons Dylan called it off, I'm going to salvage what's left and throw a humdinger of a party," she said. "No need for you to stay."

Plate in hand, she stood and turned her back on the man that drove her nuts, intending to head toward the kitchen. Mason stepped in her path, now too close for comfort.

"I'm not leaving," he said. "So you might as well tell me what you want me to do."

Mason pulled out his notebook as if to take notes.

Eyebrows pulling together, she got the distinct impression that if she didn't accept his offer to help he was going to follow her around every day until she did. Reese shifted her weight onto her heels, gaining an extra inch of space. And every little bit was needed.

"Okay, you're right," she said heaving out a sigh. "I could use the help."

And if she was really careful with the tasks she assigned, she could keep him busy enough to keep his distracting presence out of her hair....

FIVE

———

Several hours later a knock sounded in the bedroom just as Mason exited the shower wrapped in a towel, clean, and feeling human again after a nap. A nap that, in small part, made up for the insomnia and the minor migraine he'd suffered through the night before. But the expressions on the two staff members on the other side of the door left him wary.

"It's Ms. Michaels." Ethel, the gray-headed caretaker glanced briefly at her husband beside her. "We're worried about her."

Alarm rose. Reese's declaration this morning that the party was moving ahead as planned had caused more than a few raised eyebrows among the staff.

Mason still doubted the sanity of the plan himself.

"What's wrong now?" Mason asked.

"She's in the freezer," the equally gray-headed, Mr. Ethel said.

Disbelief drove Mason's brow higher.

After another sideways glance at her husband, who looked as confused as Mason felt, Ethel went on. "With a blow-dryer."

With a blow-dryer?

It was easy to understand the concerned looks on their faces given this current bit of disturbing news, news that drove Mason into action.

Hand clutched on the towel about his waist, Mason took the grand staircase of stone three steps at a time, cursing the size of the ridiculous estate. The twenty-five bedrooms might be perfect for housing your most important guests, the grounds ideal for throwing an elegant wedding, but it was hell getting from one end to the other. He could practically drive The Beast down the main hallways. A golf cart with GPS capabilities would definitely come in handy.

He rounded the corner to the kitchen, his damp foot slipping briefly in his haste, and headed for the walk-in cooler at the far end of the room. An extension cord trailed through the crack in the door, and a high-pitched whine filled the air.

Gripping the massive freezer handle, Mason gave it a pull. And there, wrapped in a sweater and jeans, a knit hat pulled down around her ears, gloves covering her hands, was Reese. Stunned, he watched her wave the blow-dryer along the base of one of the ice sculptures. The swans sat just to the left, frozen forever in a kiss that Mason thought was ridiculous seeing as how they were birds. With *beaks*.

His question for Reese seemed moot. "Have you lost your mind?"

She didn't seem to hear him, her focus on her task.

He'd told her this morning that he appreciated the pressure she was under, but he'd never expected her to crack quite this hard. Helping her with her arrangements had seemed logical while he was keeping an eye on her until her friends arrived to offer support. And he wasn't so obtuse he couldn't admit that a part of him liked being around her, resentment and insanity aside. Because when they'd locked eyes in the bedroom, Reese's hand pressed to her breast to keep her bodice from falling, he'd been hit with such a strong sensual surge it had driven him forward a step, with no other thought than to pull her into his arms.

And it was impossible to regret the action after months of mind-numbing absence of such impulses. No matter what expression had crossed his ex's face.

He tried again a little louder. "Have you lost your mind?"

She spared him a brief look but then went right on with the business at hand. "I'm trying to get rid of the names on the ice sculptures." She frowned at the swans. "And I have no idea how to separate those two."

Hand wrapped around the door handle, he cocked his hip and studied Reese. Her red sweater hugged breasts that might be smaller than he remembered, but were no less enticing. The gentle flare of her hips beneath her jeans was distracting too, encasing the just-the-right length of legs that used to wrap around him so eagerly. In the interest of forward progress, he pushed the memories away, only to get caught up in the spun gold that hung from beneath her cap. His fingers itched to twine through the strands and tug her close. To hold her *today*. But, good as the sensation felt, he shouldn't be lusting after a woman who, as of yesterday, had been set to marry another man.

And he sure as hell shouldn't be ogling one that was

clearly standing at the edge of sanity, poised to leap into the deep end for good.

Mason reached down and pulled the plug from the extension cord, and the blow-dryer ceased its relentless whining.

The resulting silence was deafening, until he said, "Are you trying to kill yourself?"

Reese pivoted to face him, her cheeks red, her lips faintly tinted blue, her teeth chattering. If she failed at the electrical shock method, hypothermia was clearly the backup plan.

"I'm salvaging what I can of my decorations," she said.

How could she sound so lucid while engaged in an act of lunacy? He eyed the electrical cord that crossed the floor at her feet.

"And if you succeed in melting the ice and it drips into a puddle on the floor," he said. "I don't think the stupid inscriptions will feel as critically important when twelve hundred watts shoots through your body."

A waft of frigid air swept up his torso, and he longed for a winter parka.

She frowned, her voice growing thoughtful. "Is ice a better conductor than water?"

He frowned, refusing to discuss physics while staring into a walk-in freezer dressed in nothing but a towel, his hair still damp. His man parts in danger of turning to ice and dropping off.

"If I'd known you were going to lose your mind over this I would have told you to cancel the party, Reese," he said, trying hard *not* to turn the frown to a scowl. He was willing to go along, up to a point. "Seriously, maybe you should. Everyone who really cares about you will understand." As she studied him, he became acutely aware, *again,* that he was wearing next to nothing. "And those that only pretend to care don't matter."

"No," she said, her grip on the dryer growing tight. "I'm going to throw the party of the century, and I am going to *enjoy* myself."

He heard the desperate determination in her tone and let out a groan, almost losing his hold on his towel, the urge to plow a hand through his hair great. "Fine," he said. "But for God's sake don't kill yourself in the process. Let's pull the sculptures out and I'll help you remove all the engravings."

"You can't." His expression must have communicated he was at his wit's end, because her words were firm as she went on. "Whatever we do, it has to take place in the freezer," she said. "I spoke with the sculptor. Every time the sculptures experience a change in temperature we risk getting cracks and impurities."

He didn't give a damn about cracks in the ice, didn't care if the swans came crashing down, their impossible smooch ending in a shatter on the floor. But clearly clinging to her goal of salvaging this party was what was keeping her going. And, seeing how being dumped just days before her wedding surely sucked, he imagined there were more unhealthy ways for her to deal with the turn of events.

"Okay." He gave in with a heave of his breath. "Just let me get changed and help you." He turned to go and then paused, shooting her a look that communicated he meant business. "Don't do anything until I get back," he said grimly. "Or I'll be stuck transforming the bloody reception into your wake and spend the next few days scratching RIP on every freakin' block of ice in here."

Her lips twitched, and then blossomed. And the first real smile on her beautiful face left him staring like a fool, indebted to the cold air drifting up the towel, cooling parts of him that threatened to erupt in flames.

And he did not want his first erection since the accident to occur while wrapped in a stupid towel. Finally he tore his eyes away and headed back to his bedroom...and the blissful absence of Reese. Because he'd just realized he didn't need the promise of her naked body beneath him to turn him on.

Her smile alone was enough.

Damn.

Twenty minutes after Reese watched Mason head out of the kitchen, desperately trying not to look at the top of a muscular butt barely covered by a fluffy towel, visions of muscle and sinew and tanned skin were still firmly implanted in her brain.

Angel wings on his rippling back permanently seared into her retinas.

She clutched her hot chocolate, the soothing warmth of the mug unnecessary. Donning the borrowed winter gear from Ethel, the head of staff at Bellington, hadn't been adequate for the twenty minutes she'd spent with the blow-dryer on a single block of ice, the process frustratingly slow. At that rate, she would have lost her fingers to frostbite before she'd finished erasing the first *Dylan and Reese*.

But one look at Mason dressed in a towel had heated her through and through. Why every block of ice in the freezer hadn't spontaneously burst into flames, she had no idea.

She enjoyed sex just fine, but why was she suddenly turning into the man-obsessed, younger version of Gina? Barely able to function during the simple act of unbuttoning her dress, her mind fried by a fuller glimpse of his toned body. Her relationship with Dylan was...had been...still might be?—Gah, she was so confused!—fairly strong. As compatible in bed as out. It wasn't an issue she'd thought much about, mostly because there was never a sense of anything lacking in that department.

So why was Mason able to affect her so much merely by existing?

The exasperated look he'd tossed her way before leaving still lingered in her mind.

Her lips frowned against her mug, and she sipped the creamy drink. She knew he thought her plan was ridiculous, but he'd offered to help anyway. And she never thought she'd actually feel grateful toward the one man who could infuriate her with a simple look.

Mason returned with a plastic tool case in hand, waylaying her thoughts. And, praise be, he'd pulled on tennis shoes, jeans and a sweatshirt with the words Semper Fi on the front.

"What's in there?" she asked.

He set the case on the kitchen counter. "Among other things, a cordless sander."

"Cordless as in it doesn't need to be plugged in?"

"Cordless as in Operation Erasure won't end in a needless death."

The tone in his voice, the spark of amusement in his eyes, almost made her smile again.

After pulling out a power tool he headed back into the freezer. Careful to leave the door propped open a crack, she followed and winced when the wall of cold air hit, enveloping her like an icy cloak. She silently watched Mason work quickly and efficiently, lifting the bottom of each bag, his cordless sander smoothing out hers and Dylan's name with an efficiency that was oddly disturbing.

She refused to ponder the karmic significance.

"How many of these ice vases are there again?" he asked.

"Thirty."

He looked at her as if he was going to pop a vein in his head.

Clearly a little more explanation was in order. "One for the flower arrangement on each table."

"Couldn't go with the standard crystal," he muttered, moving on the next vase. "Too simple for you, I guess."

Simple.

No, her wedding to Mason had been simple. Just her, Mason, the judge and his clerk as a witness. Five minutes later and she'd been Mrs. Mason Hicks.

A little over a year after that and she'd been filing for a divorce.

Their whole relationship had lasted less time than she'd taken to set a date to marry Dylan. Everything about her relationship with Mason had been fast and furious. The meeting and falling in love. The decision to marry. The sex...

And...she was slipping down that mental, bottomless hole again.

She briefly closed her eyes, forcing the image of Mason in bed from her mind.

Fortunately the cold of the freezer settled deep, chilling any lingering heat. Reese wrapped her arms around her front, trying to keep warm. But when a shiver shuddered through her, the sideways look from Mason was sharp.

"You don't need to be in here," he said. "I can take care of this."

Gratitude surged through her body, and she blinked back the emotion from her face. "I can't very well let you face the freezing temperature alone, not when this was my idea."

He let out his standard grunt. The one she could never interpret. Was he agreeing with her? Or disagreeing? Or was he simply remarking on her current state of crazy as succinctly as possible?

"The next time you decide to get married," he said, shooting her a look from the corner of his eye. "Promise me you'll use the standard crystal vases, okay. *Minus* the personalized touch."

It was hard not to be affected watching the man, his lower lip clamped between his teeth in concentration. A memory crept in, a time when she'd wanted to see a show that was impossible to get tickets to, and he'd stood in line for five hours just to ensure that she did. Funny how all the good memories had been crowded out by the bad. She swallowed hard. Clearly he was cold, stopping every once in a while to blow on his fingers, his breath visible in the chilled air, occasionally stamping his feet. Several times she offered to take over, but he'd refused, saying he was faster. And with every deleted inscription, she grew more and more grateful.

"Thanks for your help, Mason," she said.

"No problem," he said automatically.

As if his help was no big deal. And suddenly, she really needed to know.

"Why did you come?" she asked.

Mason's hands went still, and several seconds ticked by as the sander ran without the grinding sound of ice being shaved. Until he turned off the power tool and adjusted the cover on the sculpture.

He turned to face her. "Because my shrink sent me."

The words bowled into her with the power of a twelve-hundred watt electrical shock.

"Your psychiatrist?" she squeaked.

He shifted uncomfortably, either from the cold or her shocked expression, and then moved to the next ice vase, lifting the cover and turning on the sander. For a moment he simply worked on the base, the grating sound filling the icy freezer again. A sound that matched the feel of her breaths, the cold air sharp in her lungs, the emotion burning her chest.

"I haven't been sleeping well," he said.

The news made her heart pinch. Her efforts to prepare for his return from Afghanistan had included researching the common problems for returning soldiers.

She studied his profile, as if all the answers to her questions were etched in his features. "Nightmares?" she asked.

"Nope." He shook his head, his concentration purely on the task at hand. "I've simply been having trouble falling asleep. When I finally do, fortunately it's pretty peaceful." He shot her a look. "No troublesome flashbacks, if that's what you're asking," he said, and God knows she'd hounded him about PTSD often enough toward the end of their marriage.

The pause lingered until he returned his attention to the ice vase in front of him.

And just like that, he shut down again.

The grinding sound resumed, and she watched him work a moment more. Did his psychiatrist think that clearing the air between them would help ease his restless state? There was definitely something bothering him. She'd sensed the tension the moment she'd laid eyes on him in the mirror. A murky edginess that was like a barrier around the man, daring anyone to attempt to scale the heights and peer at what lived inside.

But she definitely owed him for taking care of her ice-sculpture problem.

"I left because you wouldn't talk to me, Mason."

At first she wasn't sure he'd heard her over the sander. He continued on, grinding away her name, tiny ice shards flying in all directions.

But then he said, "I didn't talk because I didn't know what to say." He let out a sarcastic huff. "I'm not much of a communicator. Never have been."

"I needed to feel like I was a part of your life. You shut me out."

The harsh laugh was devoid of humor. "Trust me," he said, "at that stage of my life, you didn't want to be inside of my head. Hell," he went on. "*I* didn't want to be inside of my head."

The words were painful to hear. She didn't want to feel sympathy or understanding, not on top of all the other inappropriate feelings he was giving her. Besides, it was too late for that.

"I wanted to help," she said.

His lips tensed, and he set the grinder aside. Their gazes locked for a moment, the ghost of the old battles they'd fought alive and churning and filling the freezer. "You couldn't." He pulled a lighter from his pocket and flicked the striker, the flame bursting to life. Holding the fire beneath the Swans' beaks, he melted the connection between the two. "Nobody could, Reese."

The old resentment flared, reminding her why she hadn't wanted to have this discussion. Were his words supposed to make her feel better? Because they didn't.

The man wasn't made to be in a relationship.

"Somebody could if you let them," she said. "And don't you see, Mason, that's how marriage is *supposed* to work."

The connection melted, the swans' beaks shorter, blunter, and Mason returned the lighter to his pocket, saying nothing.

Damn the man.

"I left everything behind to live on the base," Reese said, hating the memories. "Waiting for you to come back. I defied my family and moved away from my friends." The loneliness and the anger and the pain rose like a familiar wave. And now that she was on a roll, the words came faster and faster. "My parents kept telling me you'd never change. That I should come back to New York City while I waited for you to come back. But I wanted to create a home for the two of us."

He said nothing as he reached into the case, exchanging one tool for another.

"Do you have any idea how much I was looking forward to you coming home?" Against her will, her voice rose an octave. "To me?"

His expression inscrutable, he used a tiny electric saw to file through the ice block the two swans shared, neatly severing the base in two. The two birds were now free of each other. With slightly malformed beaks, yes, but no longer joined forever.

Which for some reason really ticked her off.

"Even when you returned from Afghanistan, it was like you didn't want me around."

"I felt numb."

Tears stung her eyes, but it was the anger that colored her tone. "I wish I could say the same, Mason. Numb would have been nice. You just made me feel like crap," she said. And she was surprised to realize how cathartic such a crass statement could be.

Mason finally let out a sigh, the first sign of emotion. "Damn Reese," Mason said, his face in a full fledge grimace of guilt. "That wasn't my intent."

She continued on, ignoring his expression. "You emotionally discarded me like a superfluous piece of nothing, and it took me months, *years* to recover."

In the frigid pause that followed, Mason slowly set the saw on the freezer shelf and turned to face her, his expression sincere.

His voice was gruff. "I'm sorry I made you so unhappy," he said. "You deserved better."

The words settled deep, soothing the age-old hurt, easing the ten-year-old festering resentment. She stared at him, intrigued by how much those simple words could affect her. Even when she hadn't realized just how rotten the leftover emotions had made her feel.

"You deserved better then and you deserve better

now." Mason blinked once, but his expression didn't budge. "Someone like Dylan."

Mason paced the obnoxiously ornate bedroom for the millionth time and glanced at the alarm clock on the nightstand.

Two o'clock in the freakin' morning.

Great.

With a sigh, he rubbed a hand down his face, feeling weary. Exhausted. And longing for sleep that just wouldn't come.

He'd learned long ago not to fight the process, because lying in bed and tossing and turning, wishing he was sleeping, was a hundred times worse than getting up and moving around. Knowing he was in for a long night, he fetched the well-worn tennis ball from his duffel bag and began to bounce it against the floor. A ritual his psychiatrist had suggested, Mason found it worked well to relieve the tension. Because the longer it took to fall asleep, the more uptight he got, and the longer it took to fall asleep.

A vicious cycle that the mindless activity helped to break.

Tired of the same four walls, he exited the bedroom and headed down the dimly lit hallway, bouncing the ball as he went. Letting his mind drift and the rhythm soothe the restless ache.

Until Reese's words slid through his mind. The expression on her face. The hurt in her eyes. He'd known how hard his absence had been on her. He knew how frustrated she'd been by his close-lipped behavior. But back then she'd been more emotionally fragile. And, in a way, he'd always feared if he'd cracked open his head and let all the nasty emotions come spewing out he would have scared her away.

Little had he known keeping them locked up tight would have the same result.

Yes, her anger he knew well—backward, forward and inside out. But what he hadn't known was how sad he'd made her. Or how she'd begun to have doubts about herself. He'd been too caught up in the chaos and confusion of readjusting to civilian life. And too frustrated by a rapidly deteriorating marriage to appreciate Reese's point of view. Each time she'd escaped to visit her parents—the family that made him feel like a fish out of water, as left out as he'd been during his school days—it had felt like a betrayal, too.

But in retrospect, he supposed her trips back home had been the only thing that had kept her grounded. His family consisted of him and his dad, and Mason had learned to be independent at an early age. A far cry from Reese's coddled existence. At the time, it had been easier to blame the clash of cultures for their problems. But even then, as much as he'd hated her parents' pretentiousness, he knew that he hadn't been making Reese happy. Knew, too, that he was starting to feel like an outsider in his own marriage as well. Blaming her mother and father had simply been a cop-out.

Mason headed down the steps, concentrating on keeping control of the ball as he went. The palatial-sized home built in the late eighteen hundreds was eerie at night, but staying inside the same four walls was no longer an option.

He just hoped he'd eventually find a way to relax.

SIX

———

Well, she hoped Mason felt better.

Because, even though she'd initially felt a sense of release to finally articulate her feelings, she'd felt good for about ten minutes. Until Mason's stunned face had slipped into one of resignation, and she'd instantly regretted dredging up the past, revisiting those dark days when she'd been so unhappy. Currently she was trying hard not to remember the look in his eyes, the disturbed expression on his face. Sleep was out of the question.

Work was her only hope for escape...even if it was the middle of the night.

Sitting in the huge kitchen, Reese took the last sip of champagne in her glass, grateful for the warmth curling in her stomach as she stared at the computer layout, trying hard not to visualize Mason in a towel and simply concentrate on the task at hand. Reviewing the list of those who had decided to come to the event, filling in the information on her seating chart. But one thing she hadn't counted on was how the wedding-that-wouldn't-be would affect who could sit where.

Reese poured herself a second glass of Dom, considering her options.

She couldn't seat her impossibly blunt friend, Gina, who had cursed Dylan on the phone despite Reese's attempt to calm her down, next to Dylan's aunt. Because Aunt Trish had never thought Reese was good enough for her darling nephew anyway. And since both women had decided to come—Gina in support of her friend, and Aunt Trish most likely to gloat that Dylan had come to his senses—they had to sit *somewhere*. Leaving the two at the same table was clearly a bad plan.

Reese gulped down half the contents of her champagne flute and sighed, welcoming the easing of the tension that followed as her mind worked on a solution.

Placing Gina next to Tuck wouldn't work either, because, although Tuck was Reese's cousin, he was also Dylan's best friend and best man. When she'd finally gotten hold of Tuck on the phone, he'd already made up his mind about how the split had played out, blaming her ex. And then she'd made the massive mistake of defending Mason—another poor choice on her part.

A vision of Mason's naked chest filled her head and a throb developed between her eyes. Reese drained her glass, feeling warm, grateful for the lovely fuzzies that were seeping through her limbs. Determined to keep thoughts of Mason at bay and turn the party into a nice evening for her friends and family.

But why had she not considered that people would take sides? Just like when the Awesome Foursome had learned that Gina had slept with Marnie's engaged brother, neatly splitting their gang of four in two. She really needed her friends by her side and, if nothing else, maybe rallying around her would bring them all back together again.

Regardless, she couldn't change her mind now. Besides, if she tried a little harder she'd come up with the perfect chart.

Reese sighed and pushed the hair out of her eyes, staring at her champagne flute and wondering why it was empty. Another glass was definitely in order; she wasn't going to get through rearranging the seating chart without it. Thank God for the multitude of boxes of champagne Dylan had ordered for the reception. She reached for the half-empty bottle of Dom Pérignon she'd stuck in the refrigerator, in case of an emergency.

This definitely constituted an emergency.

The rest was destined for Dylan's wine cellar and not for the party, because champagne was just too much of a reminder of what *wasn't* going to take place...a toast to the bride and groom.

With a tiny frown she filled her champagne flute to the top and downed a generous mouthful, her body now lazy and languid and lax.

A faint *thump...thump...thump* sounded from down the hallway. But the warmth that had been building now filled her head with a comforting cotton, and the noise that should have raised an alarm—or at least made her concerned—only registered as a dim curiosity.

With effort, and mentally cussing her clumsy finger, she clicked on the wedding photo of her and Mason, the smiles on their faces filling her computer screen. Years ago, in a fit of fury, she'd destroyed all the other photos of the two of them. But when she'd come to this one, she just couldn't.

She'd kept it as a reminder of just how far your heart could lead you astray.

For the umpteenth time that day, her mind drifted back to the breathtakingly sinful sight of Mason's butt barely covered by the towel. Breath coming faster, she reached for her champagne flute and drained the glass, rolling the bubbly over her tongue.

She scrunched her face, feeling a little unsteady, and listened to the *thump...thump...thump* come closer. And then, as if her persistent, sensual memories had conjured him up, Mason rounded the corner. He didn't see her at first, concentrating on the tennis ball he bounced as he went, a furrow of concentration between his brow, his hair sexily rumpled. Warm-up pants were slung low across his hips, and the edge of his briefs were visible. Shirtless, his torso and every delectable washboard hump on display.

Before, the visions of Mason had simply haunted her, lingering like a persistent shadow in her brain. Now they stalked her and repeatedly hit her in the chest. As if his reappearance in her life had flipped a sexual switch, turning what used to be an uncomfortable annoyance into an outright obsession.

Dear God, what was wrong with her?

Unfortunately when she finally managed to drag her gaze up from the tantalizing sight of his abs, her eyes landed on the dog tags gleaming against his skin, and her breath caught. Her head swam. The world tipped.

Her fingers clutched the bottle of champagne, as if for support, and she blurted out the first thought that popped into her head.

* * *

"Come celebrate with me, Mason."

When he heard Reese, Mason almost missed the tennis ball on the bounce up. And then he caught sight of her and nearly dropped it again.

She was sitting in the kitchen on a wrought iron bar stool at the center island, her pajamas consisting of a tank top and shorts in fire-engine red. The color went well with her fair complexion and blond hair, bringing out the pink in her flushed face—reminiscent of how she'd always looked after they made love. Her breasts were tantalizingly outlined by the silk. Her thighs exposed, her calves hooked around the legs of her chair. Too casual. Too comfortable.

And way too much skin exposed.

Heat bled down Mason's back, spread to his limbs and burned deep into his groin. He spent a moment adjusting to the sensation, mutinously welcoming its return until she released the champagne bottle and went to pick up her glass, almost knocking it over before she fumbled to fix her mistake.

Mason eyed the half-empty bottle next to her champagne flute. Damn, apparently Park Avenue had been enjoying herself for a while. The heightened color on her face was clearly from alcohol.

"Want some?" she said.

Something told him he was going to need his wits about him.

"No, thanks." He studied her warily and leaned against the doorjamb. "What are we celebrating?"

She waved a clumsy hand at the laptop. "Reworking the seating chart for the dinner," she said. "And I think

I just figured out how to place everyone so they are least likely to kill each other." He frowned in confusion, but she simply raised her glass of champagne in a toast. "So cheers to that."

He folded his arms across his chest. "Good news," he said, not really meaning the words. "That will certainly make the evening more pleasant."

Her laugh was a touch on the hysterical side. "Oh, I'm not making any promises," she said. "Because I've now officially heard back from everyone about the wedding-that-isn't. Close to three-quarters of the guests are coming to my salvaged party."

He narrowed his eyes at her. "Is that a good thing?"

"I don't know," she said honestly, blinking up at him with a look that was almost...cute. She hiccuped and went on. "I'll let you know about twenty minutes into the event."

He lifted a brow. "I'm not planning on sticking around that long."

"Well, why ever not?" she asked. "The potential for a fistfight should add some excitement. Some are coming to enjoy the party. Some are Team Reese and are here to support the poor bride." She made a face at the word *poor* and then went on. "Others are Team Dylan and clearly side with the magnanimous groom."

Mason wasn't entirely sure what magnanimous meant, but figured it was a synonym for *perfect*.

"My cousin Tuck, for one." Reese listed a bit to the left before righting herself again. "He's mad at me. But he's absolutely livid with you."

Because he couldn't think of a goddamn response to *that,* he grunted.

"Says he's coming up here to kick your ass," she went on, looking completely unconcerned with the words that fell from her mouth.

In fact, she looked faintly amused by the idea.

Great.

"I expect the rest of the guests simply want to gawk at the whole ridiculous mess." She sighed and plopped her elbow on the center island, propping her chin on her hand, the clumsy movements overdramatized thanks to the alcohol in her system. "I'm just not sure how to keep everyone from taking sides."

"Reese, I—"

"I know," she said, her face brightening with an exaggerated sense of excitement. "Maybe I can talk Dylan into coming so that me and my ex-husband and my ex-fiancé can pose for pictures together."

"Now you're just being ridiculous."

"*I'm* being ridiculous?" she said with a scowl that held no heart. "Most women fantasize about having two guys fight over her. Me?" She tapped her chest a little harder than necessary. He was surprised she didn't knock her unsteady self off the bar stool. "I get two good-looking men, each trying to shove me at the other."

Mason bit back the smile.

"I've got a fiancé—" She stopped and then shrugged, correcting herself. "An *ex*-fiancé, ushering me in the direction of my ex-husband. Claiming I need to be fair and hear you out, that you deserve to be heard. Apparently because you're some sort of hero or something."

The scoff escaped before he could restrain it.

A small furrow appeared between her eyebrows. "And

why does Dylan always have to be so damn understanding?"

It was the first cross word she'd spoken about the man, and his brow bunched in hesitation.

"Reese, I'm sure he—"

"You know," she said, her words thick. "It took him three months to convince me to go out with him."

He curled his hand around the tennis ball, hating the turn in the conversation. "He's a patient man."

"Very," she said. "I don't know why he put up with me." She paused, her voice thoughtful. "I don't know why he still does."

He stared at the tipsy woman as several answers flitted through his head.

Because she was worth the wait.

Because she was, and always had been, exceptional.

Because she was beautiful, and her touch could set a man on fire...

Mason shoved the last thought aside.

"I refused to date Dylan at first because my overbearing mother, God bless her, had been trying to set us up for years." She pulled a face. "I thought he was too perfect. And he is, you know," she went on, and Mason's gut tensed at the words. "Rich. Handsome. Big-shot corporate lawyer. Funny and brilliant. I don't know a single girl who didn't consider him to be *the* bachelor to catch."

Mason was less than excited about standing here and listening to Reese sing Dylan's praises.

But it was worse when she continued. "But mostly I said no because I hadn't quite gotten over the effects of my first marriage."

Hell, that wasn't any better as a topic for discussion,

either. And he needed her to cork her mouth before he lost his mind completely. Or worse, developed another headache.

"And then there's you," she plowed on, and Mason went still.

Preparing for the diatribe. Tensing for the inevitable show of anger. Or maybe she would list out all his failures, of which there were many.

"The ex who shows up looking good and smelling good." She frowned. "No doubt you taste just as good as I remember, too."

The heat coiling in his groin intensified. She must be drunker than he thought. No way would his ex-wife have confessed as much to the man she'd sworn she never wanted to see again.

"And then you have the audacity to help me out with my ice-sculpture problem," she went on, staring at him as if grateful, confused and angry, all at the same time. "All the while trying to convince me to win back my ex-fiancé."

She slumped a little in her seat. "Not exactly an ego booster, if you know what I mean."

He was done listening to what the loose-lipped Reese had to say.

Mason pushed off from the doorjamb. "Reese, let's call it a night and—"

"But what I can't figure..." she said, standing.

She swayed on her feet, and Mason suppressed the urge to go and steady her. She wouldn't want his help. And touching her in this state was a bad idea.

But when she reached for the bottle of champagne he knew he had to intervene, so he stepped forward and resolutely slid the Dom Pérignon out of her reach. Which had the unfortunate result of putting her too far into his personal space for comfort, bringing her golden expanse of skin closer.

Taking that personal bubble and infusing it with a heat that had his heart thundering in his chest, remembering…

"What I can't figure out—" she stared up at him with blue eyes you could lose your soul in "—is why I can't stop thinking about how it used to be between us."

Retreat suddenly went from being a good idea to one that was absolutely vital to his peace of mind. As if mocking the thought, she leaned in close, her sweet, caramel scent teasing his nose. And his libido.

"Your touch was poison, Mason." Her slurred words were delivered as easily as if she were sharing the TV listing. "But I also think I was just an inexperienced girl who didn't know any better. And—" she sent him a sloppy smile "—in the interest of science, I was hoping I could test that theory out and prove myself right."

The words tangled in a knot in his gut, and his lips twitched.

"You're drunk, Reese."

She gently flung out her arms, swaying a little, a goofy grin spreading across her mouth. "Why, yes I am," she said, and Mason bit back a smile at her adorably flushed face. "I haven't felt this good in ages. Certainly not since all my wedding plans got flushed down the toilet."

Reese stepped closer, and Mason steeled himself against the volley of sensations. The faintly sweet smell that reminded him of crème brûlée. The scent of champagne.

The sight of her parted lips.

"Aren't you tired of camouflage green?" She brushed her hand down the side of his warm-up pants, and his breath stuttered to a stop. "Certainly you must own something other than standard-issue military duds. Don't you ever want to get wild and crazy and, you know, go with a blue T-shirt instead?"

His participation tonight clearly didn't seem necessary. Because when he didn't, *couldn't,* respond, she slid her hand around his hip, dragging his pulse higher as she went, her secretive smile setting him on edge. His body shook so hard from the force of his heartbeat that he didn't notice she'd slid his notebook from his back pocket until she was dangling it in front of his face.

"And what's with the little sidekick here?" she asked, moving to flip through his notes.

He relieved her of his property, because there was no way in hell he was delving into that part of his life in the middle of the freakin' night. And with his drunk ex-wife.

Her sinfully seductive hands instantly found another target.

"And these..." Her fingers curled around his dog tags. The knuckles against his chest electrified his skin as he stared down at Reese. She cocked her head, her eyes guileless. "Are they the same ones I threw at you?"

Body humming, he considered his response. He should lie. He should tell her he'd lost them. Or, at the very least, he should tell her he got a new set somewhere along the way.

Instead, he said, "The very ones."

Tugging on his chain, she pulled his head closer. "I really need to know, Mason."

He really needed to stop staring at her mouth.

"Know what?" he said, his voice as rough as rocks on a gravel road.

"If your kiss feels the same."

She tugged him close until her softness was molded against his hard length, fitting every nook and cranny so completely that the resulting explosion in his body rivaled the sixteen sticks of C4 that had nearly killed him. And while it didn't physically knock him on his ass, mentally it might as well have.

Christ, he really needed to get out of here.

Because that long-dormant part of his body was now fully awake, and it wasn't a gentle awakening, either. More like a reflexive jerk to his feet, weapons drawn, his erection harder than the concrete he'd crash-landed against eight months ago. He froze, partly in wonder, partly in relief that he wasn't permanently afflicted with an annoyingly apathetic libido. And partly because the urge to haul her into his arms, to sink back into the heat he remembered so well—to feed the age-old *need*—was practically crippling.

Her sweet scent tantalized his nose, the expanse of creamy skin reminding him there wasn't an inch on her body he hadn't once made love to with his hands and mouth. Because he couldn't help himself, because the sensation still felt so glorious and new, he reached up and twined a lock of golden hair around his finger. The longing to tug her mouth to his, to taste her again, was overwhelming.

He leaned in close enough to feel her breath on his cheek, see her chest heaving. But the overly bright eyes reminded him that she wasn't herself. In the morning, she'd regret making a pass at her ex-husband.

Especially when she remembered she wanted to win Dylan back.

With a grunt of exasperation, he gently clutched her shoulders. "Not gonna happen, Park Avenue," he said. And while every cell was chanting to pull her closer, to taste the woman he'd pushed away years ago and celebrate his sexual return to the living, he set her back. The disappointment in her eyes was hard to watch. But nowhere near as bad as the regret would be tomorrow morning. And the fierce desire to take her again could only mean one thing.

It was past time for him to leave.

So much white. Too much like a wedding.

She had to do something.

Head pounding relentlessly, Reese cursed her stupidity for imbibing in too much champagne last night. The noontime sunshine was overly bright, birds irritatingly cheerful as they chirped. Reese shaded her eyes as she stared at the two tents that had been erected this morning while she slept off the effects of too much alcohol, tables and chairs arranged for dinner with room for dancing, as well. With rolled-up walls, the canvas structures offered a gorgeous view of the Victorian gardens and the Atlantic beyond, yet still afforded plenty of protection from the elements, should the need arise.

But they were so...so...*white*.

In fact, the glare from the sun was almost blinding, or maybe that was just the hangover. Unfortunately, most of her memories were intact. She remembered Mason showing up in the kitchen, looking all buff and gorgeous and temptingly dark. She remembered being way too free with the thoughts racing inside her head. But mostly, she remembered the feeling of Mason leading her back to her room and tucking her into bed. Like a wayward kid who'd gotten out of line.

And she might have made another pass at him. Or maybe that had been her mind working overtime in her sleep.

Because last night she'd had dreams about Mason. The same ones that had haunted her for the three rough years after her divorce. Hot images of the two of them, mostly based, unfortunately, on real-life experiences.

Pressing a hand to her forehead, hoping to ease the ache, Reese forced herself to focus and eyed the great white tents in front of her. She'd thought about all of her options, but she knew she had no choice. Since painting the canvas wasn't possible, adding swaths of color to the ceiling was her only choice to tone down the wedding-ish feel. Regrettably the sizes of the two shelters meant she needed some serious yardage. Yardage no one was available to deliver for several days. And she needed that yardage now. Which meant she had to climb into her car and make the considerable drive to pick up the fabric herself. Too bad her Mercedes-Benz convertible wasn't big enough to get the job done.

But then again, Mason had The Beast....

Reese stifled a groan. Facing the man after her embarrassing behavior last night ranked right up there with getting ditched days before her wedding. Riding in the truck where they'd first made love would be torture. Which meant her feet dragged as she started the long trek to

Mason's room, and she had to force herself to step up to his bedroom and knock.

When Mason opened the door, the first thing she noticed was that he was dressed. No bared torso with a view of the dog tags against his chest. No towel clung low on his hips. Instead, he was in a T-shirt and jeans.

So far so good.

The second thing she noticed was how glaringly tidy the room was. His penchant for orderliness seemed unnatural, despite his years in the military.

The third thing she noticed was the guarded look on his fatigued face.

"Don't worry," she said dryly. "I'm sober."

Painfully, *painfully* sober.

She parked her shoulder against the jamb hoping to appear casually unaffected. "I'm sorry about last night."

The intervening silence could have been a whole lot more awkward.

Mason seemed to be unconcerned about her inebriated come-on. "No need." A small lift of his shoulders followed. "You're allowed to blow off a little steam."

Was that what she'd been doing? Blowing off steam? Because it sure felt more like she'd been trying to seduce her ex.

"Uhh...thanks for being there for the setup of the tents," she said. "And the arrangement of the tables and chairs."

He cleared his throat. "Yeah," he said. "About that." His lips tugged up in one corner. "Originally they set up a head table for the bridal party."

Reese let out a groan.

"I had them fix the arrangement," Mason said.

She swallowed back the overwhelming swell of gratitude and then acknowledged how strange it was to have her *ex* be the one to help her out. To know what she needed without being asked. To be the one there for her when the two of them hadn't been able to coordinate anything beyond a round of sex during their short-lived marriage. Granted, she hadn't called anyone else to come and assist.

But still...

"Thanks," she said simply.

Because any more than that would have her throwing her arms around his neck in appreciation and babbling like the frazzled mess that she was.

She briefly pressed her lids closed before going on. "I know it's a lot to ask, but can you do me another favor?"

He turned and cocked an eyebrow at her, his expression reminding her of the bold, brash guy she'd met in that diner oh so many years ago.

She hurried to clarify. "And I don't mean kissing me."

The man was clearly the inventor of the indecipherable expression, and the noncommittal grunt could have meant anything.

Best not to dwell on that, so she plowed on. "I have to pick up several hundred yards of royal blue fabric today, and my convertible isn't going to cut it. I was hoping we could take The Beast."

The purse of his lips left her ruffled. "I thought you hated my truck."

"I hate any vehicle without air-conditioning," she said. "Especially when the heat index climbs above eighty."

She steadily held his gaze and ignored the memory of

the fiery temperatures the cab had reached the first time
they'd made love.

"I don't think it's such a great idea," he said.

"Please," she said.

Two heartbeats passed. She could read the tension in
his shoulders, the hard set of his lips. And yeah, she understood his reluctance.

Mason finally heaved out a breath. "Okay, let's get on
the road."

In a casual denim miniskirt and simple blouse, Reese
hauled herself up into the truck, grateful the first guests
weren't set to arrive until tomorrow. Because it meant
there was no one around to observe her less than graceful ascent. The cab hadn't changed. Same cracked leather
seats. Same threadbare carpet on the floor. And the same
faint smell of motor oil.

But when Mason cranked the engine and country
music filled the truck she looked at him in surprise. "You
fixed the radio."

"The five hundred miles I drove to get here would have
been pretty boring without some sort of company," he
said, and then shifted into gear.

And that appeared to be the extent of Mason's willing-
ness to converse. Most of the two-hour drive was spent in
silence. One hand resting on the wheel, the other draped
across the seat behind her, Mason looked lost in thought.
And it was hard not to remember how happy she'd been
in college, sitting next to him in this godforsaken truck.

By the time Mason had parked in the shade across the
street from the fabric store, the tense silence of the long
trip had left her on edge. Restless. Desperate to *move*.

And Reese hopped down from the truck with a deep need to escape the man whose presence in her life had lasted only one of her twenty-nine years, yet who seemed to hold more than his fair share of her memories.

Inside the store, she lingered longer than she should have, taking her time. As if choosing the precise shade of royal blue fabric was of paramount importance. Selection finally complete, the store owner hauled the large bolts of fabric out to the truck and set them in back. Dreading the drive and a return to their previously stilted silence, Reese rounded to the passenger side of the truck and peered in the window. Mason was propped in the corner between the door and the seat, arms crossed, eyes closed. Deep in sleep. She blinked, her breath snagging in her throat, and then entered the truck as quietly as she could.

And feasted her eyes on the man she'd once loved with her whole heart.

Long, muscular legs stretched out before him and crossed at the ankles. His biceps bulged nicely, arms folded and resting on his torso. The dog tags hanging around his neck caught the sun, gleaming in the light, shifting with every rise and fall of his chest. Thick, brown hair finger-combed into a sexy bed-head style that was— and she hated to admit it—heartwarmingly adorable. His breathing slow and easy, his body relaxed in sleep, he should have looked peaceful.

But his brow was creased with tension, and suddenly his hand twitched, as if grasping for something in his dreams.

A sinking feeling settled deep in her gut. She hated to wake him, especially while studying the faint circles just beneath the black, crescent-shaped lashes, the fatigue so clearly etched on his face. She shouldn't be wondering why the man was having so much trouble sleeping. Or why he was up pacing the halls at two in the morning when the rest of the world was asleep.

Worse, she shouldn't be wondering if he ever dreamed about *her*.

SEVEN

"Is this seat available?"

Elbows on the counter of the bustling Brooklyn diner, Mason turned to face the female behind him and was hit with an eerie feeling that cut through his fatigue. The blonde was uncommonly beautiful, both unfamiliar and yet striking a chord of recognition, as well.

Reese. How did he know her name? And why the hell did he feel so tired?

"It's available if you're trying to pick me up," he said with his most charming grin.

The wry smile that lit her lips was expected. "I'm trying to order dessert."

"Climb on up." He nodded at the empty bar stool, fascinated by the silky hair that hung to her waist. The kind a man liked to wind around his hand to hold on. "They have great pie here. I can help you pick the best one."

She perched herself on the stool and shot him a look. "I'm perfectly capable of making my own selection."

She wore sleek, high heels, a classy skirt that ended just above her knees and a flouncy blouse that looked out of place in the family-owned diner that fed the working stiffs. This chick hardly qualified.

"No apple pie for you," he said.

"Why do you say that?"

"Too normal," he said. "Too ordinary. Too girl-next-door."

And nothing about this woman was ordinary. Certainly nobody this classy had ever lived next to him.

"Pumpkin doesn't cut it," he said. "Because you don't strike me as the spicy type."

Mason liked his women spicy, so why he found her so attractive he wasn't sure.

She didn't look offended. Simply lifted a fine eyebrow with an air of tolerance. Yet Mason could sense the curiosity, too.

"Maybe you just don't bring out the spicy vibe in me," she said.

Oh, but he would. How he knew that he wasn't sure.

"Lemon meringue is definitely out," he went on.

"Why do you say that?"

"Because lemon is tart, and you're far too sweet."

He tipped his head, pursing his lips as he pretended to give the thought serious consideration. "You look like a chocolate silk pie kind of woman."

Smooth and satiny, classy and sleek. Yep, that was definitely it. And he smiled a smile that was probably goofy, pleased with his choice that matched the woman so well.

"I'm not sure if I should feel insulted or flattered to be compared to a dessert," she said.

He leaned in close, trying to track her scent to the source. Her neck? Chest? Or the lovely dip between her breasts? "Definitely flattered," he said.

"Unfortunately—" she tucked a strand of golden silk behind an ear "—you're wrong on all accounts." She turned her face to his, the blue eyes mesmerizing. "I'm really more of a crème brûlée kind of girl."

Of course she was, because she screamed money, and pie was way too middle class.

He shot her a grin. "I know." And then he frowned, a strange uneasiness spreading through his chest. "Why do I already know that?"

Reese's face grew confused, as if he'd said something he shouldn't have. Like she'd been handed a script that was wrong or had been changed at the last minute, no one checking with her first. Odder still, why did he crave the kiss that he knew with one hundred percent certainty would taste like crème brûlée?

And then they were in his truck, and Reese was pressing her soft body against him, and Mason was struggling to keep from mauling her mouth, afraid he'd scare her off. Because his lips moved against hers with a hunger that seemed old and timeless and etched with a deep-seated frustration, as if he'd waited forever to taste her. But he'd just met her, so how could that be?

And how had they ended up in his truck? With his hands fisted in her hair? But then Reese arched against him, and he decided he didn't care how the hell they'd wound up here. He was just glad they had. Out of place and time, the cabin dark, the night beyond darker still. And as he dropped one hand to her thigh, sliding her skirt up to her waist, he knew they were going to make love. His nerves leaped and vibrated with delight as he traced smooth skin, felt her softness and her warmth and her silk.

And the urge to take her burned too bright, too hot for such a short acquaintance.

It was as if he'd been here hundreds of times before, yet it felt like the first time, too.

"Mason," she breathed against him, and he pushed the confusion aside and allowed himself to slip deeper into the sensual fog, awash in the pleasure the woman brought.

And he had the sinking feeling that, once they made love, his world would never be the same again.

She whispered something against his mouth, a feathery softness that was such a tease, urging him on. Encouraging him to go faster, before they ran out of time.

Sensing an urgency he didn't understand, he tried to shift her closer, but the fatigue made every movement thick, every thought heavy as he fought to open his eyes, battling to lift the lids that felt soldered shut.

And when he finally succeeded, there was Reese, leaning over him again. Same worried look on her face. Same tantalizing blond tresses, but when had she cut her hair?

And why had she stopped kissing him?

Brow delicately furrowed with concern, she touched his shoulder. "Are you okay?"

Afraid she'd escape again, afraid he'd suddenly shift to a location that didn't contain this woman who smelled of caramel and tasted like a rich dessert, he threaded his fingers through her hair and hauled her lips down to his.

Struggling to make sense of what had just happened, Reese froze, her head swimming at the sensation of being back in Mason's arms. One minute he'd been sleeping and the next he was awake—his gaze shifting from confusion to hunger in a flash—and dragging her close. And when he pulled her firmly down against his hard chest, his lips on hers, her body sighed with the memory.

She had a fleeting thought of Dylan. Of regaining her sanity and pushing Mason away. But then he breathed her name against her mouth, a sound that was full of so many memories, so many emotions she couldn't begin to sort them all. And then, as if needing skin on skin, he dropped his hand to the dip in her lower back.

Mason arched his hips, his erection firm against her belly, and Reese pushed all reason aside, instinctively doing what Mason had trained her to do....

Respond.

She gripped the muscles where his neck met his shoulder, her fingers twining around the chain of his dog tags, and threw herself into the embrace. Returning his kiss with a fierceness of her own, born of the hundreds of nights she'd dreamed of this very thing. For three years she'd regretted throwing those dog tags at Mason. Despite the piercing pain of his desertion, she'd questioned her decision to demand a divorce. She'd doubted her ability to move on. And she'd longed to be back in the arms of the man who made her feel like no other.

And now here she was, confirming that the memories were nowhere near as good as the real thing. He slanted his lips across hers, lifting up, then pressing down, followed by a small circular motion. As if seeking just the right sweet spot. And as they settled deeper into the kiss, he drew her in and in and *in,* until the sensation of falling was overwhelming.

Mason rasped his tongue across hers, and she responded in kind, canting her head up to accept more.

One hand in her hair, he slid the other to cup a breast, flicking his thumb across a tip. Pleasure sluiced through her and she stretched against him, seeking better contact with the man she'd craved for years.

In a way she was grateful to know the consuming attraction wasn't one-sided, because when she'd thrown herself at Mason last night, and he'd pushed her away, a small part of her had withered up and died. Frustrated by the thought that she was the only one who still felt caught in the web of desire. Angry that she was the only one having difficulty putting the spark behind her.

Her mind kept screaming he was quicksand.

And she kept remembering his response, "but what a way to go..."

Across the street a car horn ripped through the air, and Reese jumped, returning to reality with a crash.

"Mason," she said, pushing him away. "This isn't real."

Which was a stupid statement, because *of course* the kiss had happened. But, yeah, she wasn't exactly capable of logical thinking right now. Not with the way her body was shaking as if it had just brushed the frayed end of a live electrical wire.

For a moment, Mason looked confused, his lips ruddy, kiss-bitten and damp. And so damn sexy her heart bled a little. But then he sat up and dragged a hand across his mouth, shifting higher in the seat.

"Well, it sure as hell felt pretty real to me," he said.

And while her body screamed *yes* her mind screamed *retreat.*

"N-no," she stuttered. "I mean..." What did she mean? "This chemistry between us. It's..." Her voice died again as she fought to come up with the right words. But after ten years, she *still* couldn't give it a name. "It's just that. Chemistry. Based on hormones."

Which sounded so ridiculous and inadequate and trite that an embarrassed rush of heat joined the fire already fanning her face.

"Hormones?" he said, underscoring the ludicrousness of her statement.

She lifted her chin and said nothing.

His hazel gaze bored right through her, as if reading the truth in her heart. "Whatever gets you through the night, Park Avenue," he said, turning to start the truck.

And she turned to face forward, certain that the next two hours were going to feel like twenty.

Once he'd parked The Beast in the drive of Bellington Estate, Reese had scattered faster than buckshot from a shotgun, and Mason headed straight for his room. He needed to finish packing. He needed to get out of here.

Because if he didn't escape soon he feared it would be too late.

As he crossed the foyer, a fierce stab of pain shot up his head and settled behind his left eye, sending a spark of lights across his vision.

Great. The perfect end to the perfect day.

He'd made a fool of himself in the car. And while he could blame the whole scenario on his fatigue and the screwed-up dream of his and Reese's first meeting—a weird mix of memories of the past and flashes of the present—well...he knew better.

Now that he'd tasted Reese again, keeping his hands off her would be impossible. As far as he figured it, currently they were about half a bottle of champagne away from winding up in bed together. And since his ex-wife was still extolling the virtues of her ex-fiancé, it was a clear signal that it was time for him to leave. He didn't care how much like a wedding reception her party was going to be or how many yards of fabric she needed for the tent, he was getting the hell away from Bellington Estate.

As he headed up the grand staircase, the ice pick knifing him in the base of the skull mushroomed to the size of a metal poker. One that had just been pulled from a fire. Adding a searing sensation to the relentless stabbing that was punishment enough on its own. As the ache turned to agony, Mason picked up the pace. If he could just get to his room and lie down everything would be okay.

One foot in front of the other, Hicks. One foot in front of the other.

But the internal chant became useless when he finally reached the second floor and turned down the hallway. Dizziness hit with a force that brought him to a halt.

Head swirling, Mason reached for the wall to steady himself. But his aim was off and he missed. Thrown off course, he lost his balance, sinking to all fours.

"Damn," he muttered.

Beads of sweat popped along his brow. His body grew damp from the relentless spinning.

Lids closed, his eyes jerked in a saccadic movement he couldn't control, as if the freakin' merry-go-round in his head would stop if he could just fixate on a solid point. He blindly reached for the wall, hoping to steady himself as he stood. But the attempt only brought a wave of nausea, the urge to vomit so strong he collapsed to the rug, hugging the carpet on the floor. Desperate for relief. Praying for the spinning to cease so he could climb off the torturous amusement park ride in his brain. But the rpms only increased. And Mason let out a groan.

Because there was no way in hell he could make it to his room now.

When Reese rounded the corner to the main hallway, she stumbled over Mason's body, and her heart nearly leaped from her chest to the floor. Scrambling to maintain her balance, she dropped to her knees to the floor beside him.

"Mason, what are you doing?"

This was followed by his standard grunt, and, despite the turmoil his presence was currently wreaking in her life, she was grateful he was alive.

"Studying the priceless oriental carpet," he said, his voice strained. "Hell, Reese, what do you think I'm doing?"

He turned his head, wincing with the effort as he looked up at her. "You think I want to be sprawled on the floor? Because I have better things to do than count the number of fibers per square inch in the carpet."

"Can you stand up?"

"No," he groaned. "Too dizzy."

In all the time they were together, she'd never seen him exhibit even a hint of weakness, taking the strong, smart-ass attitude to the extreme. Seeing Mason lying on the floor, unable to get up, was disturbing. But she ignored the small part of her that was panicking.

"What do you want me to do?" she said.

"Help me to my bed."

She pulled on his arm, straining to half help, half pull him to his feet.

Jeez, his body did more than look rock solid. There wasn't a smidgen of fat on him, so how much did all those muscles weigh? And then he swayed and she had to brace her legs to keep from collapsing under the load.

No easy task.

When she'd finally managed to get him to his feet, he listed alarmingly to the left, and she gripped his hard chest, more than a little concerned about his condition. Not to mention the delicious hum of her body in response to the muscles beneath her fingers. She shifted her hands to his narrow waist, felt the jut of his hip, and then searched for a hold that didn't elicit such a flood of sensual images in her head. Unfortunately, her attempt was a failure.

Because in the truck, the feel of his hard body had just about done her in.

"Do you think you can walk?" she asked.

"Normally, yes," he said dryly.

How could a man in such pain be such a smart aleck?

"But these goddamn migraines get me so dizzy I can't stand," he said. "And when I do, I usually throw up." He sent her a look, his face pale with pain. "Don't say I didn't warn you."

"Duly noted." She looped his arm over her shoulder and staggered at the burden. "How long have you been having migraines?"

"Ever since an IED exploded, knocked me on my ass and nearly killed me."

Her heart chose this moment to finally plunge to the floor, and she sucked in a breath at the thought of Mason dead.

All that cocky arrogance...wiped away.

All those dry, smart-ass comments...gone.

There would be no more annoying, noncommittal grunts to try and interpret. No more irritating habit of being helpful during her moment of humiliation. And certainly no more kisses that were so hot they could melt an ice sculpture from twenty feet away.

While still housed within a walk-in freezer.

"Damn it, Mason," she said, her lips tight from the emotional and physical strain. "Why didn't you tell me?"

But she knew why. Because, no matter how many years had passed, Mason Hicks was as incapable of sharing his life now as he was ten years ago. Stupid, *stupid*, man.

"You should have told me," she said, frustration driving her volume higher.

The grimace on Mason's face was sharp. "Not so loud, Park Avenue."

Instantly, she winced. "Sorry," she whispered, feeling helpless and hopeless and out of her depth. Just like he always made her feel. "You'll have to tell me how to help. I've never known anyone who has migraines."

"Not much to know. Just treat me like I'm hungover."

She shot him a curious look, not following his comparison.

His attempted smile was pathetic, and she hated feeling so sorry for him. "Until I sleep it off, don't talk too loud. No bright lights," he said. "And above all else, keep your distance. Because I have the annoying tendency to toss my cookies without warning."

But keeping her distance was impossible as they spent the next ten minutes hobbling their way to Mason's room. The journey felt like forever. Clearly dizzy, Mason had to use her for support, and keeping him upright wasn't easy. Worse, he was starting to look a little green around the gills. She focused on his bedroom door, praying her strength would last long enough to reach his room. And when he finally did get sick, they'd just managed to make it to the bathroom.

Unfortunately they hadn't quite reached the toilet.

Mason used the tile wall to hold himself up.

"I'm sorry, Reese," he said, his face deathly pale. "First I attack you in the truck, and now this."

Remembering how he'd made her feel in the truck wasn't helping her remain calm.

"What do you need?" she said.

His brow beaded with sweat, his shirt damp with exertion, he said, "A hosing off would be nice."

She opened the shower door remembering how much they'd both needed a hosing off in his truck today. "Just so we're clear, I think the word you're looking for is 'ravage' not 'attack.' And second—" she turned on the water "—if I had my choice, I'd prefer being kissed to cleaning up vomit."

Without shame, Mason parked his shoulder against the wall and shucked his clothing, clearly in too much pain to worry about modesty. After all, they had spent plenty of time naked in each other's presence. Ten years shouldn't make a difference.

But it did. Especially now that she had such a blistering-hot, present-day memory to add to the old. Jaw clenched, she helped him into the shower, forcing her eyes to remain on the pained expression on his face. Ignoring all the tempting tanned skin on display, the gorgeous masculine and very muscular frame brushing against hers.

She propped him against the tile, her dry throat eased by the steam from the shower.

Hand braced against the wall, his head bowed as the water sluiced down that beautiful body. She did her best to ignore the thighs of iron, the ripple of muscles and sinew in his back, the angel wings tattooed on his shoulders.

But when she noticed the black marking on his butt, her eyes went wide, the taut backside sporting the number sixteen.

"You have *two* tattoos," she said, feeling dumb.

He was a Marine after all.

And as she stared at his tush, her mind fought to remain functional. *Sculpted* shouldn't be the word a person uses to describe the part of the human anatomy built for sitting. And slowly she realized her comment had just given away the fact she was ogling his butt.

She ripped her gaze away and back to his face.

But Mason was in too much pain to care.

"Got them both after I nearly died," he said.

Her heart contracted as he uttered the words again. No need to ask what the angel wings represented.

She blinked back the emotions the thought brought. "What does the sixteen stand for?"

"The number of sticks of C4 that forced me to come face-to-face with my beliefs in an afterlife."

Silence fell between them, and, finally, it was too much.

Reese deliberately turned away from his beautiful form, forcing herself to attend to the mess on the floor. Hands shaking, she worked quickly and quietly, using the cleaning supplies she'd found under the bathroom sink.

Unfortunately, the task didn't take her as long as she'd predicted. And there was no relief from the thoughts whirling in her brain.

Because not once had Mason complained about his insomnia. Not once had he complained about his debilitating headaches. And he sure hadn't shared that he'd come so close to dying.

The thought of him suffering alone, not wanting—or unable—to ask for help had her insides churning so hard she feared she might get sick, too.

Steeling her nerves she pushed the thought aside. Mason was alone because Mason *chose* to be alone.

When she'd finished her task and he'd finished his shower, she handed him a thick towel, and he tucked it around his waist. And while she helped him to the bed, she vowed not to let her eyes wander anymore.

No getting sidetracked by the vulnerable Mason.

No being distracted by that gorgeous display of male anatomy.

They reached the far end of the room, Reese drew the bedcovers back, and Mason sank onto the mattress, closing his eyes. Sultry dark lashes fanned just above the dark smudges that were now more pronounced. His face taut with pain, she just resisted the urge to kiss the scar on his temple. To smooth the puckered skin with her fingers. She closed her hand into a fist.

He's just an addictive drug, Reese.

A delicious drug maybe, but a drug nonetheless. And she couldn't afford to let herself get sucked up into his world again.

"Thanks for helping me out," he said, his voice rough.

"I'll stick around. Just in case you need me again."

"Not necessary, Park Avenue." He didn't bother opening his eyes. In fact, he seemed careful not to move his
head at all. His face drawn, Mason Hicks looked out of
place amidst the peach comforter and matching silk
sheets. All those manly muscles attached to the lost-boy,
tousled look and surrounded by luxurious bedding. "Your
guests arrive tomorrow," he said, his attempt at a smile
lame. "You should go."

And without his help, the party would have been a
disaster. Because she'd been so caught up in salvaging
her pride by putting her best foot forward, she hadn't
stopped to think how much of a wedding reminder every
decoration would be.

All of which seemed petty and superficial and unimportant given how this man had almost lost his life. And
how much that life had been affected by his injury. She
hesitated, fighting the self-protective need to flee and
the irresistible urge to stay.

"Why didn't you tell me about your headaches?" she
said.

The responding shrug was small, as if it were no big
deal.

But pain that intense was incapacitating.

"Hell," he said roughly, "I'm luckier than most. Some
returned home minus a limb. Some returned missing several." He paused for moment. When he went on, his voice
was low, weary. "And some never made it home at all."

She blinked back the sting of tears, finally hearing
the words she'd needed to hear ten years ago. But he'd
come to terms with all of that without her. Because he'd
refused her help.

"That doesn't mean the pain you're suffering doesn't

matter, Mason." He would brush it off as no big deal. He brushed everything off as no big deal, even when it was. Stoic till the bitter end, even during the final days of their marriage. *Especially* during the final days of their marriage.

"Go get some rest, Reese," he said.

She propped the pillows on the opposite side of the bed. "I'm not going anywhere." Careful not to jar the mattress and cause Mason even more pain, she moved his duffel bag to the floor and took its place on the bed, adjusting her denim skirt on her thighs. "I'll stay until you fall asleep."

His lips twisted. He clearly was unhappy she was insisting on sticking around.

"I hate being seen like this," he said.

Her eyes drifted over his bared chest, the ripple of muscles and the flat abdomen. A dark dusting of hair tapered to a V, disappearing beneath the towel draped low across lean hips.

She swallowed, trying to force more moisture into her mouth.

"Being seen how?" she asked.

"Helpless." His voice lowered a notch. "Weak."

She studied Mason. "Everyone needs to lean on someone now and then," she said. She'd learned that when she'd leaned on Dylan in the years following her divorce. And her divorce probably wouldn't have happened if Mason had leaned on her after his first tour in Afghanistan. But that was a long time ago, and they were both different people now.

A reality that left her feeling a little melancholy.

Staring at her hands, she flicked a nail, searching for

the right words. "You know, ten years ago," she said. "I wish..."

She glanced at him again. His face was finally relaxed, his breathing deep and easy instead of hitched with pain.

Mason had finally fallen asleep.

EIGHT

———

This time, Mason was sure he was dreaming. The sweet smell of Reese seeped into his consciousness even as his fingers twitched against silken skin. For a moment, he didn't move, relishing the feeling of being rested, of holding Reese.

Before he woke up and reality crushed his happy space.

But the fragile feeling remained intact when Mason opened his eyes and found himself face-to-face with Reese. Fast asleep, she looked peaceful, her hair fanned across her cheek. She was still wearing the simple blouse and denim skirt from their trip to the fabric store. His hand rested low on her thigh, as if he'd gone to make love to her in his sleep and then remembered he didn't have that right anymore.

A single bedside lamp lit the room, the night dark beyond the window. The clock on the bedside table displayed the time: 1:00 a.m. His head no longer throbbed, but had reduced to a dull ache, and the dizzy feeling was gone. He felt foggy, drugged, but more rested than he had since he'd landed at Bellington and first seen Reese looking breathtakingly beautiful in her magical gown. As untouchable as the day she'd hurled his dog tags at him and told him to get out.

Because, despite having said I Do, a small part of her had always remained beyond his grasp. Aloof. All that class and privilege creating a barrier he hadn't really felt he'd ever breached.

But last night she'd finally broken the princess image. Despite the searing pain in his head, the gut-wrenching nausea, he'd been acutely aware that she'd stayed, cleaning up the mess he'd made when he got sick. The Reese he remembered hadn't quite known how to navigate a middle-class world. For the short duration of their marriage, her parents had paid for a maid service.

But this Reese was more...down to earth.

He spent a long minute enjoying the creamy skin of her face, the lush lashes that currently hid the bluest eyes he'd ever seen. Careful not to wake her, he swept the hair from her cheek. Although he hated someone witnessing him in the throes of one of his migraines, he was glad it had been Reese.

And then she opened her eyes, the shocking sky-colored gaze so close his mind went blank for a moment. She didn't look surprised to see him near enough to touch. She simply folded a hand beneath her cheek.

"What were you dreaming about in the truck today?" she said.

Surprised by the question, he answered without hesitation. "You."

Her lids stretched wide, and he decided he needed to clarify. No sense in revealing he had sex dreams about his ex. The truth wouldn't help.

"About our first meeting in that diner in Brooklyn," he went on.

Her smile was instantaneous. "When you proceeded to try and match me with a dessert."

"The very one."

The tiny grin was impossible to restrain. He'd been so green back then. Young. Reckless. Falling at first sight. A stupid concept, that, but he still remembered looking into her gorgeous eyes and knowing with a certainty he wasn't sophisticated enough to communicate that his life had just changed for the better.

And it was hell coming to grips with the fact that he'd come close to ruining hers. After a lifetime of being coddled and protected and indulged, she hadn't been prepared for day-to-day living, much less being married.

Especially to someone like him.

Elbow on the pillow, she propped her head on her hand, and he rolled onto his back so it was easier to look up at her. Moving his head during a migraine was like picking his way through a minefield, and right now he didn't want to tempt the Fates. Plus he didn't want to waste a moment of the opportunity to study the woman.

"Back then, I had the overwhelming urge to debate the perfect dessert to describe *you*," she said.

His brow bunched in suppressed amusement. "Why didn't you?"

"I didn't want you to think I was flirting with you."

"But you *were* flirting with me."

She rolled her eyes, and he tried not to find it adorable. "I was hoping not to be obvious about it."

"Park Avenue," he said, his voice rough. "I could sense your intentions the moment you sat on that chair."

"I wanted dessert," she huffed with feigned indignation. "And it was the only seat available."

"That's not true," he said. "There was one next to the old guy who came in every day at noon for his coffee."

"Well," she said, staring at her hand as she picked at the fabric of the sheets. "Can you blame me? I bypassed the eighty-year-old with the unfortunate habit of muttering to himself and chose the handsome guy with the ingrained cocky attitude."

His lips twitched at one corner. "I wasn't always cocky."

Her gaze shot to his. "I find that hard to believe."

"Let's just say—" he pursed his lips, searching for a way to soften the reality of the less-than-confident guy he'd been "—after years of shifting from school to school and never really fitting in, I didn't hit my stride until I enlisted in the Marines." He let out a small scoff. "It's common knowledge that boot camp breaks you then makes you."

Her eyes softened at the corners, as if in discovery.

"So," he said gruffly, finding her all-too-seeing gaze as chafing as desert sand in his skivvies. "What dessert would you have chosen to describe me?"

"That's easy. The Mason I first met would be molten lava cake."

For a brief moment, his breath froze in his throat, but he forced himself to exhale as she went on, oblivious to the effects of her words.

"Our marriage would best be represented by rocky road ice cream," she said dryly.

Mason couldn't help it. A small chuckle escaped.

"And today's Mason?" he said. He couldn't think of a

dessert with the word *dysfunctional* in the title. "Deep-fried Twinkie?"

To represent the fried state of his brain, or the nuked remains of his life.

"I know the tattoo on your shoulder should suggest chocolate angel torte," she said. "But I think devil's food cake is probably more apt."

He dipped his head in acknowledgment, until she went on.

Her gaze steady, she said, "Of course, the molten lava cake is still very applicable."

Images filled his head. Of the first day he'd arrived, standing close to Reese as anger burned in her gaze. The mesmerizing blue eyes. The enticing figure a vision in white. And images from their kiss, the desire in her face that had sent a surge of pleasure up his spine.

He paused as her statement seeped even deeper, the subtext stirring his libido. The age-old desire always seconds away from consuming him.

"Careful," he said as need settled in his groin. "I'm naked beneath this towel."

"A fact I'm well aware of."

"Me, too," he said with a wry tone. "Because it places me in a vulnerable position."

In more ways than one.

But she'd already seen him weak, prostrate, unable to walk. Unable to stand.

"Vulnerable position?" she said. This seemed to amuse her. "Once you vomit in a woman's presence, there's no going back to being the paragon of strength."

His brow crinkled in amusement even as he grimaced. There wasn't anything remotely funny about their situation. As the smile faded from her face, her eyes held his with a force that felt as if it was testing his strength.

And he was tired of reminding himself that she wasn't his anymore.

"Reese," he said, his voice gruff. "If I kiss you again, I won't stop."

An expression of acceptance settled on her face. "I know."

The two-second pause stretched into three.

"So I suggest you go to your own bed," he said.

The night seemed to pause, holding its breath in anticipation of what the woman would do. And when the words finally came, disappointment cinched his heart so hard it almost hurt.

"You need more than just two hours of rest," Reese said softly. "Go to sleep, Mason."

Several hours later, Reese woke to the heavenly feel of Mason's muscular thigh draped across her legs, her denim skirt bunched around her waist. Her blouse had crept up to her breasts, leaving her midriff bare where strong arms were wrapped around her, spooning her from behind. The towel had come loose from his waist, and his erection lay heavy and hard against the bare skin of her back.

Struck dumb, she was incapable of sending messages to her muscles to move as desire streamed up her limbs— both from the naked man pressed against her body and the embrace that was so...*proprietary.* To date, the one thing she hadn't allowed herself to remember was the way Mason had made love to her.

As if it was his God-given right and no one else's.

Clearly not awake, Mason muttered something incoherent and pressed his shaft more firmly against her, a silent demand that infused her belly with a searing heat that spread lower. Seeped between her thighs. Leaving her hot and damp and full. Preparing her for what came next.

Her body saying *yes* before Mason had even coherently asked the question. Before Reese had fully contemplated her answer.

He muttered something that sounded like her name. And, as if on instinct, his hand drifted lazily inside her blouse to cup a lace-covered breast, and she closed her eyes at the thrill, knowing she should wake him. Working up the strength to leave his bed.

Because just what was the protocol for sleeping with your ex a mere twenty-four hours before your wedding-that-wasn't party? An event that originally had been planned to celebrate her marriage to another man. What was the socially acceptable time frame between breaking up with your fiancé and sleeping with your ex? When did you cross that invisible line between being justified in your long-suppressed passions, sympathetic in your weakness for the husband you'd tried so hard to forget, and…just an unforgivable bitch?

Her chest seemed to shrink, making breathing difficult as she fought the warring factions. And while she lay there, desperately trying to make herself do the right thing, Mason made her decision that much more difficult.

Burying his nose at her neck, mumbling something she couldn't understand, Mason let his other hand drift south. Calloused fingers found their way between her legs. Desire surged through her veins, leaving a burning ache where he stroked. One hand caressing the tip of her breast, the other stoking the fire higher.

Was he still half asleep, or did he know what he was doing?

And if not, how could a man take her to such heights, leave her shaking with need, without being completely conscious?

Blood pulsing through her body, she couldn't move, even as she berated herself for the inability to push him away. Weak when faced with the potential of placing herself in Mason's hands. The thought alone had her spreading her thighs a touch, but the submissive move, the hint of acquiescence, was enough to spur Mason on.

His hands never left their targets as he rolled her onto her stomach, his hard body now stretched atop the back of hers. The muttering that followed was impossible to understand, slurred consonants and vowels that spoke of need and want and longing. And she knew without question that Mason was still caught in that no-man's land between hazy dreams and harsh reality.

Just as he had been when he'd instigated that searing kiss in The Beast.

Hot breath on her neck fanned goose bumps across her skin. Which was difficult enough to ignore, but then he pressed his straining shaft to the silk-covered heat between her legs, as if demanding she let him in. Pleasure clutched her and shook her in its grip, her body now insisting she comply.

A part of her feared that if she gave herself up to his plan, he'd be doing more than acknowledging the past, he'd be marking her future.

But those *hands*...

Those magical hands were stroking her breasts through the lace and creating a tension between her legs that was prohibitive to logical thought. His fingers dipped deeper between her folds, as if testing her response, her readiness. He rocked his erection firmly against her, communicating with his body what he wanted to happen next. And the silky slickness between her thighs had to be a major clue to what he was doing to her body.

Even when young and inexperienced, she'd known that making love to Mason would be unique. He never failed to deliver on the searing sensual promise in his hands. A passion she'd never quite achieved without the man she'd divorced.

And the need to experience that passion again was what prompted her to make up her mind.

Gripping the covers, she arched her back, signaling her response. Allowing him entry. There was a split-second pause before Mason dropped his head to her cheek, his voice scratchy from the remnants of his dreams, a sexy rumble in her ear.

"Reese."

She wasn't sure if there was a question in there or not. She had the fleeting impression there was, so she pressed her buttocks more firmly again his length.

Now clearly awake, with no further hesitation he swept the silken crotch of her panties aside and plunged between her legs.

Despite his sleep-drugged movements, the thrust was deep. No hesitation in his possession. The tight pressure brought a slash of pleasure so acute she let out a moan, a sound so shattered she closed her eyes. But there was no denying how much this man affected her.

"Reese," he repeated.

This time there wasn't a question at all, simply a statement of ownership.

As he began to slowly rock into her, he made her body sing a song she'd learned years ago, one she'd spent years trying to get out of her head. The recurrent tune relentlessly playing in her mind. And though she'd successfully hit the mute button, the melody had never truly been silenced.

One touch from Mason and it blared louder than ever before.

The sensation left no room for her to respond to that one-word demand that said little, yet meant so much. And the more time that passed, the more awake he became. Until he shifted his grip, fingers clutching the insides of her thighs as he plunged deeper, each time taking her completely. Gone was the languid rock of his hips between her thighs, the indolent air that soothed the edges.

Nothing but raw need drove him now.

She pressed her lips together as he made love to her like she remembered. The same way she experienced in her dreams. With a fierceness that stole her breath.

Skin hot and damp against hers, he nipped her neck, leaving his mark. Staking his claim. Pressing her forehead to the bed, she clung to the covers, as if she could hold on to this moment forever. Arching her back. Urging him to hurry. But Mason wouldn't be rushed.

Instead, as the intensity began to build, he paused at the end of each thrust, allowing them time to savor the feeling. The delicious ache grew so acute she stopped trying to stifle the sounds coming from her mouth. Until, one hand still curled around the inside of her thigh, he used the other to spear his fingers in her hair, turning her head to the side to meet him face-to-face.

"Reese," he said again.

Neither question nor statement, this time the word was a command.

She opened her eyes and met his heavy-lidded look. The hazel gaze lucid, yet hazy with desire. And then his mouth was on hers, lips demanding. His tongue hot and hungry, his *body* hot and hungry, he consumed her from behind, the heavy length of his hard chest pinning her to the bed. Sweat slicked their bodies. Corded muscles in his thighs pressed between hers. Every hard roll of his hips taking her with a totality that left no room for thought.

This is what she remembered best about making love to Mason. The feeling of desire that was primal, elemental. Pure hot need that seared her with his mark, as if her body had been copyrighted, branded and registered under his name.

The building ache between her thighs left every nerve thrumming with pleasure. The promise of completion just out of reach. Reese bit back a whine and arched her back, a silent plea for Mason to end the torture of dangling the promise of bliss just out of reach.

In response, one hand in her hair, he slid the other between her legs, stroking her sensitive clitoris even as he bucked harder. Faster. His mouth against hers, he groaned, coming with a hoarse cry that filled her ears. Pleasure gripped her so brutally, so fiercely, she choked back a cracked cry and shattered into a million tiny pieces that could never be repaired.

With Reese relaxed and satisfyingly boneless beneath him, Mason absently threaded his fingers through her hair, his pulse pumping as the sound that had ripped from her lips still rang in the room.

Damn.

He slammed his lids tight, but he couldn't shut out the fact that he'd just realized what he'd craved the most about making love to Reese. At her first broken moan his heart had contracted, his stomach had dipped and his chest had hitched, his mind flooding with the memories of how easily he'd been able to take her apart.

How quickly she'd come undone in his hands.

Despite his lackluster libido after the explosion, a small part of him—the part he'd been working hard to ignore—had known they'd come back to this. Reese, in his bed. He wondered when the sense of inevitability had settled so deep. When he'd unbuttoned her wedding dress, or when he'd kissed her in the truck? Had he known this would happen before he'd shown up at Bellington Estate?

Hell, maybe he'd agreed to his shrink's suggestion because he was hoping it would.

No answers came as his muscles slowly released one by one, Reese's body partly trapped beneath his. And the position made him realize that he hadn't really given her time to change her mind. To ensure that she wanted to make this move. But patience had been impossible. When she'd arched her back in a move that was purely instinctive, just like that his good intentions had been blasted to smithereens.

He'd dreamed of her this way for far too long.

Because the only way to survive the long nights of his deployment had been to pull out all the delicious memories of Reese, scrolling through them one by one. If they'd been housed in a book, the edges would be dog-eared, the pages well-worn by now.

But tonight...tonight had been even better.

An intense, hard ride that savored every thrust as if it might be their last. Clueless as to what came next, Mason knew this might be all that he'd get of Reese.

The thought had him tightening his arm around her waist and burying his nose in her neck. She didn't belong to him anymore, but he pushed that thought aside.

Because for the rest of the night, she was his.

The third time Reese woke up, the sun was shining and Mason was gone.

She bolted upright in bed, her eyes frantically scanning the room before landing on his duffel bag, still on the floor where she'd tossed it last night.

With a sigh, she flopped back against the pillow, relieved he was still somewhere on the estate, and pushed aside the niggling fear that she hadn't been sure. That she'd just slept with her ex-husband but had doubts about whether he'd even stick around for the awkward morning-after meeting. Slowly, she let the rest of the emotions roll in.

Hating that she felt happy and hopeful and horribly scared out of her mind. Just like when she'd first met the bedeviling man.

Jeez.

Stretching her arms over her head, she took in the smell of sex and sweat. The feel of rumpled covers in the bed she'd shared with Mason, the delicious ache in her body reminding her of the night in his arms. No man had ever made her feel as needy, abandoning all hope of appearing less than completely wrecked when he made love to her.

Every touch destroying her from the inside out.

They'd come together two more times last night. Each time he'd reached for her in the dark and she'd been helpless to refuse him anything. Without a sound, he'd taken her with a fierceness that was mind-boggling.

Being the focus of his efforts had left her writhing on the bed, gasping for breath and shaking with need. Shattered in the aftermath of her orgasm. There'd been no words. No discussion. No insistence they rehash the past and where'd they'd gone wrong. Of course, one touch from the man and her body craved his again with a strength that was embarrassing, despite the circumstances that loomed beyond the bedroom door.

Her guests, and Dylan's—her ex-*fiancé*, for God's sake—pending arrival.

Not to mention the hopeless nature of her relationship with Mason.

And while none of that had mattered while a naked Mason was making demands of her body, in the full light of the morning everything came crashing down, crowding in and threatening to suck her back into his world.

Quicksand. He's quicksand, Reese.

A thick, seductive quicksand that's guaranteed to take you down a second time.

Squeezing her eyes shut, Reese silenced the whispered warnings in her head. No man had ever affected her in the same way. But was that because Mason was the only man who rang her bell so loudly? Or because she'd deliberately set out to make sure that everyone else failed?

And it was disheartening to realize that, while there

was some validity to the latter, the former appeared to be true, as well.

She'd deceived herself for so long she'd bought into the lie. Making Dylan suffer, as well. And she owed it to him to tell him the truth. He needed to know that he'd been right to be concerned. Because no matter what eventually happened between her and Mason, she couldn't continue to fool herself that marrying Dylan was the right thing to do.

She needed to tell him she'd made her choice...and it wasn't him.

Not a conversation she was looking forward to.

Desperate for some soothing, she rolled out of bed and padded barefoot to the shower. Once inside, she leaned her head against the tile wall, letting warm water sluice down her back. Ignoring the memories of angel wings rippling over muscle, the tattoo announcing the number of sticks of C4 that had almost ended Mason's life.

Reese allowed herself ten more minutes to freak out before getting dressed and going down to face the rest of her day.

Marnie and Cassie and Gina were set to arrive, and, given how things had ended, their reunion was sure to be fraught with tension. She believed sorting through the current mess that was her life would leave no room to dwell on any lingering resentments between Marnie and Gina.

At least she hoped it would. Because she didn't have the mental fortitude for *too* much peacekeeping today.

A day that included welcoming guests that had originally planned on witnessing her wedding and finalizing the details for tomorrow's party. But what good came of separating kissing swans and sanding names from ice sculptures if all the guests were asking what had just happened? Especially when the only appropriate answer was one she couldn't share.

Mason Hicks had just happened.

And, as usual, after his arrival in her life...there was no going back.

NINE

"What the hell is going on, Reese?"
Standing in the sun-filled driveway next to Cassie, Gina
shot Reese a look of concern before pulling her in for a
quick hug. The brunette's British accent was tinged with
doubt as she eyed a workman in overalls as he passed by.
"I hear you're still planning on having this party."

"Yes, I am."

"That seems risky," Cassie said.

"Everything's going to be fine," Reese said with more
courage than she felt.

Fortunately, Reese had plenty to keep her mind off
her worries.

The caterer was due to arrive for their meeting, and
the gardens were crawling with extra staff building temporary wood floors for the tents. Of course, it would have
been nice if they'd arrived two days ago as originally
planned, because the incessant pounding was hardly
soothing. And she *really* needed soothing.

Unfortunately, next on her list of things to do was a
heart-to-heart with the man she was supposed to have
married tomorrow. Dylan was set to arrive anytime, mak-

ing the drive in from the city to pick up some childhood photos of him that his mother had lent to the wedding planner.

She eyed the buzz of activity going on around her.

Hardly the perfect time to let him know they were through, but she just couldn't stomach the idea of having the discussion over the phone. And she couldn't stand living with this sick feeling a moment longer. The thought of confronting Mason for the morning-after discussion was stressing her, as well.

It was then that Reese noticed that her two friends were staring at her anxiously.

Cassie's brown hair framed a face free of makeup. "I don't see the logic in throwing a party for a wedding that didn't take place."

Reese struggled for a response. Because, as the day grew closer, running from the mess she'd made of her life was beginning to feel like an attractive alternative.

"I think it's a bloody brilliant idea," Gina said.

Reese decided not to call her out on the forced optimism in her tone, addressing Cassie instead. "Not everything is about logic and numbers, Cassie."

Sometimes it was purely about stupidity.

Twisting her lips wryly, Reese linked arms with the two women and led them through the front door, grateful they were here. "So, yes, the party is still on."

Aiming for the sitting room, she steered them across the foyer. And while the house had always exuded a peaceful serenity before, now the sounds of construction echoed down the hallway.

"With everything that's happened, you never did tell me why you called me three days ago," Gina said.

Three days. Had it really only been *three* days?

"Oh, yeah. That..." Reese's breath heaved uneasily. "It's about Marnie."

The awkward pause that followed stretched to uncomfortable lengths, their footsteps joining the sounds of hammering from outside. Gina and Marnie hadn't spoken in years. Not since Gina's confession that fateful last night together.

Reese tightened her grip on their arms a bit.

"Actually," Reese said, "I called to tell you about Carter, Marnie's brother."

Gina's voice sounded hoarse. "I remember who Carter is, Reese."

Of course she would—she'd slept with the man.

While he was engaged to Marnie's childhood *friend*.

Reese cleared her throat. "He's divorced now."

After everything Gina had gone through, Reese hadn't wanted her to hear the news from someone else. Especially not from Marnie. Gina needed time to prepare. Because if she heard the report and reacted without forethought, her response might ruin the fragile truce Reese was desperately hoping for.

It took several seconds for her friend to speak, her voice careful.

Too careful.

"Why would you think that concerns me?" Gina said.

"Well, after everything that went down..." Reese released their elbows and came to a halt, shifting her eyes nervously to Cassie. But the woman simply sent her a weak shrug. No help there, so Reese went on. "Especially between you and Carter—"

"That was a million years ago. Who the hell cares?"

Gina said with a smooth smile that didn't quite reach her eyes. "You don't seriously think I've been carrying a torch for Carter, do you?"

Reese bit her lower lip and decided it was best not to give an honest response.

"It was just one night," Gina continued. "What happened, happened. I moved on a long time ago."

"Okay," Reese said. "Good..." She resumed her trek down the corridor. "So how about you two help me with the truffles?"

Falling into step beside her, doubt furrowed Cassie's brow. "Why do your truffles need help?"

"Because right now they are set to adorn each plate in containers designed to resemble engagement ring boxes."

Gina winced. "Well, that would be in bad taste."

"Exactly," Reese said. "Which is why I need help fixing the problem. Marnie will be here soon to help, too."

Gina's footsteps slowed.

After another worried look at Cassie, Reese pulled on Gina's arm. "Come on, it'll be fun."

Fun?

Nerves had her babbling nonsense now, but she knew the reunion would be a hundred times worse for Gina and Marnie. All those years ago, the news of Gina's impulsive one-night stand with Carter hadn't been received so well by his sister, to put it mildly. At the time, although Reese had maintained a neutral stance, secretly she'd wondered why Gina hadn't been able to control her urges.

After last night, Reese realized she had no business tossing those judgmental stones.

They rounded the corner and entered the antique-adorned room overlooking the beautiful Victorian garden. A container with two hundred faux wedding ring boxes graced the middle of the floor, a pile of shimmery cellophane squares and royal blue ribbon stacked on the coffee table.

"Good Lord," Gina said as she sank onto the rose-colored French settee. The brunette stared at the mountain of boxes, a defeated look on her face. "This is going to take forever."

"Not forever," Cassie said as she sat next to Gina, reaching for the box on top. After a few moments, she finally managed to undo the bow and dump the truffle onto a square of cellophane. "With two hundred boxes at approximately forty seconds per truffle, it will take roughly two and one quarter hours." She cut a piece of ribbon and tied the truffle closed, the bow a little crooked. "But with four of us, it will only take about thirty minutes."

God bless Cassie and her practical nature. Gina didn't look convinced as she silently reached for Cassie's truffle and adjusted the bow so it looked more presentable.

"The thirty minutes will turn into an hour if you get picky," Cassie said dryly.

"I say we just eat them all instead," Gina said. She shot Cassie a look and let out a sigh. "And no, I don't want to hear how long that would take."

"Why are there two gorgeous guys playing basketball outside?"

The three women were up to their elbows in truffles when Marnie appeared in the sitting room doorway, delivering her question with her classic drawl. Reese's heart briefly stopped pumping, paralyzing her muscles.

She should have been concerned about greeting Marnie properly. She should have been worried about her friends' first meeting since the breakup years ago. And she definitely should have been donning her peacekeeping hat, looking for ways to ease them all through a reunion that was bound to be awkward.

But her pulse was too erratic to provide enough support for such a complicated mental process, and all her worries boiled down to one.

Oh, God. Had Dylan arrived and challenged Mason to another game of basketball? Did Dylan sense the change in Mason? Had Mason told Dylan about last night?

Doubtful, but the possibility brought fear to Reese's heart.

She needed to be the one to tell Dylan.

Last night was *her* responsibility.

Her heart planted itself in her throat and refused to budge, and she leaped to her feet and raced toward the door, ignoring Marnie's, "What is going on?" followed by Gina's, "Beats the hell out of me."

For the millionth time, Reese cursed the size of Bellington Estate. Her heels tapped along the endless hallway as she hurried toward the side entrance, praying she wouldn't slip on the marble floor. She was vaguely aware the rest of the gang was following along, firing off questions she wasn't capable of interpreting, the worry too great.

Marnie, petite, blond, and with a lingering Southern twang, looked concerned as she quizzed Reese as they went. Gina, tall, brunette and beautifully attired in a chic pantsuit, was looking a little too intrigued by the man situation. Or maybe she was just grateful to leave the truffle troubles behind. And Cassie, in jeans and a T-shirt, had a look of forbearance. As if she was used to the melodrama, but, despite her genius IQ, still didn't quite get what all the fuss was about.

Somehow Reese always knew it would come to this. A showdown between Dylan and Mason.

Karmic justice, she was sure of it.

When Reese finally pushed through the side entrance, she came to a stop on the sunlit stoop and the rest of the Awesome Foursome clustered around her, all staring across the brick driveway.

Because there, engaged in a contentious game of one-on-one, was Mason. Only he wasn't joined by Dylan, but by Tuck, her cousin and Dylan's *best friend*. The man she'd arranged to sit next to Cassie because he was so firmly Team Dylan that Reese was worried he'd get into a verbal sparring match with Gina.

Of course, it never occurred to her he might actually get into a fistfight with Mason himself.

A strange sense of déjà vu settled over Reese. Both men were sporting jeans, both were shirtless and both had bared chests gleaming in the late-morning sunshine. But this game wasn't like the first. Because Tuck, being a former quarterback star, took competition seriously. There was no such thing as a friendly game of anything. And the two looked like they'd been going at it for a while, both hot, sweaty and with twin expressions of grim determination.

For a brief moment, Reese enjoyed the mind-boggling masculine vision of Mason Hicks.

Gina was the first to speak. "Well, isn't this just like old times? The four of us ogling men at a sporting event," she said. "We should pause to give this moment the reverence it deserves."

Tuck dribbled closer and then turned to make a jump shot.

"Check out that bum, ladies," Gina said with a whistle. "I think I've just died and gone to heaven."

Reese bit back the smile.

There was a moment of silence as they watched the two gorgeous men play. Mason secured the ball and turned, angel wings on display as he went in for the layup, and Marnie's twang filled the air.

"Which ass would we be talking about, Gina?" Marnie said.

Gina and Cassie turned surprised faces at Marnie.

"Well, well, well," Gina said, a smile creeping up her face. "I guess the sweet Southern girl is all grown-up now?"

"Who is that lovely man with your ex, Reese?" Marnie asked, as if to change the subject.

"That's my cousin, Tuck. Dylan's best man," Reese said, and then her stomach twisted. "Or he was supposed to be the best man. Now he's here for the party." Reese nibbled on her lower lip and watched Tuck elbow Mason in the side, blocking a jump shot a little more aggressively than necessary. "But I think he decided to come so he could confront Mason."

Or kill him, she wasn't sure which.

Mason retaliated with a shoulder to Tuck's chest as he dribbled by—or bulldozed by, was more like it—and landed a layup. And perhaps she should explain her cousin's state of mind.

"Tuck is mad at me," Reese said.

"It's not your fault Dylan called off the wedding," Gina said, and then her tone grew sharp. "And isn't it just like a man to tell you he loves you and then decide you're too stupid to make up your own mind about whether you love him back."

Reese's stomach sank lower. Two days ago Reese would have emphatically agreed with Gina.

Now she wasn't sure of anything anymore.

Reese blew out a breath. "But my cousin thinks Dylan wouldn't have called off the wedding if I hadn't given him a good reason."

And if her actions prior to Mason's arrival weren't enough, last night had cinched the deal.

"And so Tuck blames Mason," she finished.

Silence again after that as the four watched the two men race down the court, a magnificent show of gorgeously ripped abs, raging competitiveness and hot-blooded testosterone. Tanned skin. Sweaty bodies. And sculpted muscles. What followed was a flurry of limbs and hips and torsos fighting to gain control of the ball.

"Should we stop them before they kill each other?" Marnie drawled.

"Heavens, no." Gina shaded her eyes, as if to better take in the view. "I say we let them work it out between themselves," she said. "Your ex has gotten even hotter with time, Reese."

Unfortunately, yes he had.

Glancing at the angel wings on Mason's shoulders, Reese remembered the sixteen on his backside, now covered by low-hanging jeans as he dribbled and elbowed his way across the driveway. And while she could appreciate him paying homage to the number of sticks detonated the day he almost died, a more appropriate tattoo would have been C4, the explosive itself. Everything about the man was explosive, especially the way he made love.

"And how difficult for you that he showed up just days before your wedding," Gina said.

Three pairs of eyes stared at her with concern...and an underlying question. In their own way, each one had been there for her through her divorce, available by phone all hours of the day—and even in the middle of the night. They knew how hurt she'd been, and how getting over Mason had taken hard work. Through the years, every one of them had listened patiently as she'd vented the leftover anger directed at her ex.

"Definitely difficult," Marnie agreed softly. "You deserve your happy ending with Dylan, honey."

The weight of the truth pressed heavily on Reese's chest. They were all being so supportive, so understanding. So sweet to loyally take her side without question. Of course, they didn't know what had happened last night. And it was painful to receive all that support when she really didn't deserve it.

She needed to tell them the truth about her and Mason.

But she needed to tell Dylan *before* she shared the news. He deserved to be the first to hear of her...of her... activities with Mason.

Reese rubbed her brow, a faint tremble in her fingers.

"Though completely wrong in his assessment of the situation," Gina finally went on. "At least your cousin is quite delectable looking."

As usual, Gina could always be counted on to maintain her personal priorities.

Reese shifted on her feet. "I originally had Tuck sitting next to you at dinner, Gina. But I figured you two might be a little too outspoken to keep your opinions to yourselves."

"Too right," Gina said.

"So, in the interest of world peace," Reese said. "I moved Cassie next to Tuck."

They all watched Tuck barrel by Mason, almost knocking the man to the ground.

And Cassie, brilliant brainy Cassie, spoke her first words since they'd landed on the stoop.

"Great," Cassie said dryly. "I get to sit next to the dumb jock."

TEN

———

Body aching, muscles burning, Mason leaned against the basketball pole, his chest heaving as he struggled to catch his breath. "Truce?"

Tuck braced his hand against his side as if in pain. "Truce."

The man's dark hair stuck to his damp forehead. The bright sunshine was warm, heating Mason's sweat-slicked back. The score even, no winner had been declared. Unsatisfying, that. The only consolation was Tuck appeared just as whipped as Mason felt.

Their battle had begun when Mason had run into Reese's cousin in the driveway, and Tuck had suggested a game of one-on-one. Mason had tried to ease his way out of it, but the man wouldn't take no for an answer. Finally, feeling restless after his night with Reese, Mason had decided that a little hand-to-hand combat disguised in the form of sport might just be the release he needed.

The look on the man's face had clearly communicated his displeasure with Mason. As if Mason needed a reminder of the current FUBAR state of affairs. Tuck hadn't had much to do with him while he was married to Reese, the athlete too wrapped up in his career as a professional quarterback. There'd been no time to concern himself with his Park Avenue cousin and her husband. Interestingly enough, Tuck appeared to be concerned now.

And unlike the game with Dylan, which had consisted of two men cautiously assessing their opponent, the battle with Tuck had been satisfyingly fierce. Every jab in the abdomen, every shoulder to the chest and every aggressively blocked jump shot had eased Mason's sense of unease, and communicated Tuck's displeasure with Mason's presence.

Imagine how angry he'd be if he knew Mason had slept with Reese.

A full minute ticked by, silent save their labored breathing.

"They're good people," Tuck said.

It didn't take a college degree to figure out who he was talking about.

Mason clutched the basketball tight. "Yes, they are."

"They deserve better."

"Yes, they do."

And then Mason had appeared and blown everything all to hell.

Ironic given that his job had been locating and diffusing IEDs.

Frowning, Mason wiped the sweat from his brow as discontent burned in his gut. And while making love to Reese came as natural as breathing, in the harsh daylight, with the activity of the staff preparing for the wedding-that-wasn't party, it was harder to justify his actions.

"I didn't show up to cause problems," Mason said, hating that he sounded as if he was making excuses.

He'd come with the hope that addressing his past would help make his future better. Unfortunately, his headaches had gotten worse. His memory wasn't any better, either. But, despite their activities, last night was the most restful sleep he'd had since the accident.

"Well, unfortunately," Tuck said, "problems followed you here."

Mason shoved an agitated hand through his hair, leaning back on the balls of his feet. "I suppose my arrival did kinda shake things up."

Tuck scowled. "Thank you, Captain Obvious."

"Sergeant."

"Huh?"

Despite the stifling atmosphere, Mason's lips twisted ruefully. "Technically, that would be Sergeant Obvious."

An amused scoff burst from Tuck's mouth, and the sudden light in his eyes eased the tension-filled air. In another time, another place, Mason would have liked to have bought the man a beer. He respected the man's loyalty to his friend. And he respected the way Tuck preferred to express himself via a full-contact, bone-jarring game of one-on-one.

The kind of communication Mason preferred himself.

"Are you two done trying to kill each other?"

At Reese's voice, Mason turned to watch her cross the brick driveway. She certainly didn't look like a woman who'd spent the night engaged in sweaty, steamy sex. Heat curled in his stomach like a contented pet, the memories threatening to make him do something foolish. She was beautiful as ever in a pink skirt and matching blouse that appeared to be made of silk. The shade close to the color of her lips, and reminding him of cotton candy. Soft.

Sweet. The kind of sugar that melted on your tongue and seeped straight to your blood.

Next to the Park Avenue Princess, as usual he felt like an outsider.

She came to a halt in front of Mason, Tuck just to his left, and shaded her eyes as she looked up at him. There was a question in her gaze that he couldn't answer. Which was why he'd never turned on the lights last night. As much as he'd wanted to feast on the sight of her naked body, especially after dreaming of her for so long, he just couldn't stomach seeing the look in her eyes.

The questions he knew that would follow.

And he was no closer to the answers than he'd been ten years ago.

So, instead, he'd avoided the inevitable inquiry and poured himself into making love to Reese.

The spring breeze cooled the sweat on his brow and the moment turned awkward. Reese staring at Mason. Mason staring at Reese. And Tuck, the animosity oozing off the man as he watched the two of them. The pounding hammers of the workmen in the garden filled the air.

"Just what is going on between you two?" Tuck said.

A pit opened beneath his stomach, because damned if he knew—outside of a night of trying to make up for ten years of not making love to Reese.

As if that were even possible.

Reese's mesmerizing blue gaze never left Mason's. "It's none of your business, Tuck."

Tuck's scornful scoff echoed off the brick driveway. "The hell it isn't," he said. The man took a step closer. "Reese—"

"I need to speak with Mason, Tuck," Reese said, turning her gaze to her cousin. "Alone."

And while Mason hadn't been particularly thrilled with the man's presence before, suddenly having him around seemed like a good idea. A heck of a lot better than facing Reese, especially when she looked ready to buckle down for a discussion.

With a sigh, Tuck plowed his hand through his hair. "Fine," he said. "I'm off to take a shower."

A few seconds passed before Reese nodded at Tuck's retreating back. "He's a fiercely loyal friend. And that takes precedent over a straying cousin."

"Loyal is good," Mason said.

But misplaced loyalty was bad. The kind of loyalty that meant you couldn't let go of the woman you once promised fidelity to, no matter what the divorce decree had stated. He hadn't been chaste in a physical sense. Hell, he was as red-blooded as the next guy. But, even before the accident and its libido-killing effects, the women had been few and far between. And not one of them had meant much; none coming anywhere near the realm of replacing Reese.

In retrospect it had been easy to blame it on his lifestyle. The decisions he'd made and his commitment to the job. Being married to the Marines had been his choice, and he was well aware it wasn't easy on the loved ones in your life. History was full of failed military marriages, and the reasons were many: the long separations, the stress of the job. The way the work could screw with your head.

But after last night all his rationalizations had been blasted to holy hell.

He hadn't moved on because he was still hung up on his ex-wife. And not just in a sexual sense.

Damn.

"We need to talk, Mason."

"Not much to discuss."

Her hurt expression was frustrating. "I just—" She paused, obviously searching for the right words.

Mason wasn't sure there were any.

Trying again, Reese said, "After last night—"

The roar of a car engine interrupted, and from down the driveway Dylan's Jaguar came into view.

"Ahh," Mason said, hating that he sounded, *felt*, bitter. "The return of Mr. Perfect."

"I..." Reese coughed as if to clear a sizable object from her throat. "I have to speak with Dylan."

The words burned through his chest, leaving him angry, frustrated with himself for the reaction, and with a terrible sense of inevitability.

"Yep," he said in a low voice. "You sure do."

Her blue eyes grew bigger and she stepped closer. "Mason—"

But then he turned on his heel and left her behind, pointedly ignoring the Jag as it pulled up and parked.

Reese finally managed to get Dylan alone out by the gazebo in the rose garden, waiting patiently until his phone conversation ended and he stuck his cellular in his pocket. He looked tanned and fit and as good-looking as ever in his custom-tailored suit.

"You didn't have to drive all the way here for these," Reese said as she handed him the manila envelope she'd retrieved from her car.

The packet contained the photos the event planner had left Reese.

"My mother wants them back," Dylan said as he tucked the envelope under his arm. "They're the only ones she has of me with my grandfather." His gaze was easy on hers. "And she didn't trust them with anyone other than me."

Reese's translation? The woman didn't trust her ex-future-daughter-in-law. Certainly not now that the wedding had been called off.

She shifted her weight on her hip, feeling antsy. Nervous. "The family display of pictures would have made a nice addition to the wedding reception."

Especially with both sets of parents pleased their children were set to tie the knot. She knew her mom and dad had always wanted the union, and Dylan's family had been just as enthusiastic. Which meant any relationship with Mason would be considered the ultimate betrayal by both sides.

She pushed the daunting thought away.

Dylan went on. "I had no idea Mom had enlisted the help of the event planner to set up the display as a surprise for us."

The news gave her pause. "Your mother has been in touch with Claire?" Reese said.

"Apparently they've been having weekly phone chats since you hired her."

Reese's mouth fell open, remembering Claire's suggestion for the music for their first dance. And wondering why the woman had even cared.

Reese huffed out a breath. "Well, that would explain

why it always felt like Claire was working for someone else."

Probably because she had been. Reese wouldn't put it past Dylan's mother to try and use her considerable influence to sway the wedding plans in a direction that would meet with her approval. As the matriarch of the Brookes dynasty, she was used to being Queen.

"It also explains why Claire didn't want me to move forward with the party," Reese said.

Dylan rubbed his neck. "To put it mildly, Mom's not exactly in favor of the idea."

Reese was beginning to have doubts herself. But she couldn't back out now, especially the day before the event. Because the only thing *worse* than a canceled wedding was a canceled-wedding-turned-party-event which ended up being called off, as well. Reese would wind up looking like the ultimate flake, unable to make a decision.

Unable to make up her mind about what she wanted.

She eyed Dylan, her gaze traveling over his handsome face. One thing was abundantly clear to her now.

"I can't marry you," she blurted.

The pause was long, and Dylan crossed his arms, settling his back against the gazebo. Pink climbing roses threaded their way through the slats of the trellis, infusing the air with their scent. He looked remarkably calm about her statement. Come to think of it, he always looked remarkably calm.

Despite *his* composure, Reese's heart tripped faster.

"You were right." She pushed herself to go on. "I had some things to resolve."

She stared out across the grounds of the estate, the

perfect location for the perfect wedding to the perfect man. And Dylan was as close to perfect as she'd ever met.

"Mason," he said, and there was no question in his tone.

She blinked back the surge of anxiety, inhaling deeply to gather her courage. But she'd lied to herself so often through the years. That she was ready to get married again. That she was simply taking her time to get the special day just right. And that she was over Mason...

Dylan had been right, and she had been wrong, and she just couldn't keep lying anymore.

"I slept with him."

Silence fell between them, heavy and stifling. Dylan's mouth slowly twisted, as if he were biting back his words. When his eyes briefly returned to hers, his gaze churned with an emotion she couldn't read.

"You know—" he huffed out a small, disbelieving laugh and shook his head "—when I canceled the wedding and told you to go figure out what you wanted, that wasn't what I had in mind."

"I'm sorry."

She stared at his profile, the words building in her chest until they had to escape. "Are you angry?"

He pursed his lips, scanning the gorgeous view as if searching for an answer to her question.

Until another scoff escaped. "I should be, shouldn't I?" he said softly.

Stunned by his words, the clashing emotions threatened to drag her down. Happy he wasn't angry. And...sad he wasn't angry. Because his response beamed a bright, harsh spotlight on all that hadn't been right about their relationship. She'd gotten it all wrong.

Again.

"We were good together, Reese. We made a great team. And our families were certainly happy with us." Dylan sighed and stepped closer. "But I'm glad the decision has been made," he went on. "On paper, we look like a good match." He swiped a hand through his hair. "But in real life..."

The silence that followed was full of meaning.

She tried, and failed, to swallow past the swelling in her throat. "Then why did you ask me to marry you?"

"I'm sick of the dating scene, and I'm at the point in my life where I'm ready to settle down," he said with a small shrug. "And I knew I could spend the rest of my life with you and be perfectly content."

"Content?"

Dylan hesitated before going on, and the words that followed hit her hard. "Taking care of you was never hard, Reese."

Taking *care* of her?

Stunned to the core, Reese watched Dylan straighten, as if ready to bring this conversation to a close.

"I know you wanted to put this party on," he said. "But honestly, I'm not in the mood to hang around and social-ize." His eyes searched hers. "Are you okay to handle to-morrow by yourself?"

His concern was genuine.

Taking care of you was never hard, Reese....

Had she really been leaning on him so much? Reese blinked twice, struggling to adjust to the new point of view.

Her voice felt raw. "Is that why you tried to talk me out of moving forward with the party?" Her brow bunched as she tried to process his surprising reactions. "Because you thought I wouldn't be able to handle it?"

The expression on his face said it all.

"That's why you came out to pick up the pictures yourself," she said, the truth finally settling in like a humiliating lodestone around her neck. "Because you were worried and wanted to check up on me."

In response, Dylan simply linked his fingers with hers. A familiar gesture they'd shared more times than she could count. One that had comforted her, made her *feel* comfortable. Reassured. Cared for. She'd just never realized that they weren't truly partners. Because with partners came a give and take.

Apparently on her end it had been mostly take.

She had leaned on the man during the months following her divorce. She'd definitely moved from grateful friend to contented girlfriend. And maybe they had settled in a little too fast, satisfied with the easy relationship. After the turbulent days of her marriage, it had been nice not to have work too hard. For life to fall into place easily and without a lot of effort. But, in retrospect, the flip side of that meant that she wasn't growing. In this case, she wasn't even sure she'd been dealing with reality.

"Eventually we'll need to discuss your future at the foundation," he said. She nodded numbly. "But we can talk about that another time."

He squeezed her hand, leaning in to kiss her cheek before turning and heading up the walk toward the driveway. Reese stared after him, wondering how her life had managed to change so much in just a few days.

And how had she been so off about their relationship? Was she destined to go through life completely clueless?

With that thought, she whirled on her heel with the intent of seeking Mason out...and promptly ran smack into his bare chest.

T-shirt slung over his shoulder, jeans hanging low on lean hips, he gripped her elbows, and she was immediately overwhelmed. By the calloused fingers on her skin. His heat. His intoxicating, manly scent that evoked delicious memories. And all that glorious, glorious expanse of skin stretched across muscles, his chest damp from exertion. Thickly fringed hazel eyes glanced from Reese, and then at Dylan's retreating form.

And when Mason set her back, the look on his face was hardly reassuring.

Although his heart seemed to pump an excess of blood with every thump, Mason managed an unaffected expression during the strained pause that followed. At least he hoped he did.

And then Reese blurted, "I was talking to Dylan."

He cocked his head, a small part of him vaguely amused she was stating the obvious, but the amusement didn't last long.

As he'd stood there watching Dylan with Reese, their fingers linked, the sincerity in their expressions had nearly done him in. But the slump in her shoulders as her ex-fiancé left was the worst. In that moment in time it became abundantly clear that, not only was he still hung up on his ex-wife, he resented the hell out of her ability to move on.

He hadn't been able to, but Reese...Reese had gone so far as to get engaged.

She'd already told Mason that she loved Dylan. And,

heck, they'd been divorced for ten years now, so reason suggested he shouldn't be bitter about the fact that she'd managed to get over her ex. Even if he'd been too messed up to manage it himself.

But reason wasn't really his specialty right now.

Especially as the memory of the last time he made love to her rolled through him with all the subtlety of a thunderstorm. Mason had laced their hands together, Reese had wrapped her legs around his waist and the moment had felt so right. Almost...perfect.

The burning ache in his gut grew, a twisted compilation of anger, resentment and pain that felt like a tangled pile of C4, just waiting to go off.

"We need to talk," Reese said.

Her expression upped the stifling pressure in his chest.

He wasn't thrilled about the idea of picking apart what had gone down last night. Certainly not with this churning pile of emotion roiling in his gut. The sound of the carpenters constructing the temporary stage for the DJ was loud, pounding hammers echoing in the air. Two workers passed by, taking the shortest path between the driveway and the tents.

"You left this morning without waking me up," she said.

He turned to meet the brittle gaze that reminded him of the ice sculptures he'd modified for tomorrow's party, and his tone held a finality that he couldn't disguise. "I'm not the one who was set to get married tomorrow."

Her lids fluttered wide. "Mason," she said, "I'm not—"

"Reese!"

Gina's voice cut through the air, and Reese groaned.

"The DJ just arrived to set up his equipment," Gina

said. The worried look on the brunette's face, her British accent heavier with the strain, didn't bode well for the interruption. Her gaze briefly touched on Mason's before returning to Reese. "Have you seen the list of his songs?"

Reese stared at her friend. "I emailed him an amended list."

"I don't think he got the requested changes," Gina said.

"What do you mean?" Reese asked.

Gina cocked an eyebrow. "Because I asked him which song he was going to lead with tomorrow." The tiny furrows on Reese's brow grew deep as Gina continued. "'Marry Me' by Train."

Which would have been hilarious except for the pressure in his lungs that was making every breath sting. Like he'd just played a game of one-on-one with Michael Jordan himself.

Reese groaned. "Clearly communicating by email is out. I can't have the man playing every romantic song on the original playlist."

Because that would make the groom's absence abundantly clear, a reminder of the canceled wedding with every tune. Mason bit back the scowl. Whatever this was between them, whatever lingering leftovers of their relationship remained, he needed to remember that Reese would have gone through with the ceremony if Mason hadn't showed up and Dylan hadn't backed out.

The throb starting at his temples didn't feel like his usual migraine, but the pain was no less intense.

"Great." Reese briefly covered her eyes with her hand, inhaling deeply, and then dropped her arm to her side. "Tell the DJ I'm coming," she said to Gina, who took off, presumably to do exactly that.

Reese turned to Mason, who wanted to be anywhere but here, looking into those baby blues. And when she clutched his wrist, the touch shouldn't have burned so deeply. "I have to go talk to the DJ," she said.

Instead of asking her to stay, or questioning her about what she was trying to accomplish with this bloody party, he managed a "hunh" in response. Her grip turned harder, and he hated the look that washed across her face. The one that clearly communicated "we're not done having this discussion."

When they'd been married, he'd *despised* that expression.

And his patience had just run out.

He peeled her fingers from his arm.

"Do the right thing, Reese," Mason said, setting her back. "Go chase Dylan down and tell him you're sorry, that we were a mistake." He held her gaze a moment more before going on, knowing, finally, that he was doing the right thing. "And then tell him you're ready to work on fixing your relationship."

She pressed her lids closed, replacing deep blue with a heavy fringe of dark lashes. When she opened her eyes again, her gaze was firm. "Mason," she said. "Don't. Go. *Anywhere*."

And then she took off in the same direction as Gina.

Mason's standard grunt following her directive hadn't been reassuring, and a rising sense of confusion and fear meant her words were firmer than she'd intended. It was this same sense of urgency that had Reese scrambling inside and up the stairs to her bedroom for the revised playlist. Unfortunately, it took her ten minutes to make her way through the endless, antique-adorned halls to her bedroom, retrieve the amended list and then hunt down the DJ in the tent. And if speaking with him face-to-face and handing him the paper personally wasn't good enough to get the requested changes, she might have to hurt someone.

How was she supposed to juggle her man problems with so many people around? The next time she was dumped days before her wedding, she wasn't going to try and carry on with the party as planned. And if she *was* forced to suffer a disastrous repeat of the past, she was going to make sure she wasn't left juggling two exes at once.

The sound of the construction ringing through the air scraped on her last working nerve as she impressed upon the DJ the importance of sticking to the new list. Finding Mason again was her next priority. But as her search turned up nothing, she grew frantic.

He wasn't outside. He wasn't on the first floor. And he wasn't in his bedroom. Worse, his duffel bag was gone. Muscles stretched tight from the tension, Reese knew where she needed to check next.

As she headed past her bedroom, she grabbed her keys, and was out of breath when she finally arrived back at the front hallway. Of course, given that she'd probably run half a mile this morning just making her way around the castle-sized estate, she had good reason to be feeling winded.

Unfortunately, despite her speed and the risk to her neck in her high heels, it took her another minute to make her way out onto the driveway.

And by that time The Beast was gone.

ELEVEN

———

Stunned by the discovery, unable to focus, Reese dashed down the front steps and almost ran over Gina, who was standing next to Cassie and Marnie.

"Your gorgeous ex just took off in that ghastly red truck," Gina said.

"Did he say where he was going?" Reese wheezed out.

"He didn't say anything at all," Gina replied. "Just passed by looking all grim and moody."

Reese let out a scoff. She was feeling pretty grim and moody herself.

She shot her friends a plaintive look. "Can you go find the caterer and tell him I'll be late to our meeting?"

Marnie looked concerned. "Reese—"

Reese flew across the brick driveway, making a beeline for her car. As she opened the door to her Mercedes-Benz, she knew her three friends were looking at her as if she'd misplaced her mind somewhere along the way.

"Where are you going?" Gina called after her.

"After Mason," she said, and jumped into her car.

If her friends asked her why, she didn't hear them as she roared off. The beautiful grounds of the hundred-

acre estate flew by as she headed up the winding driveway to the highway.

Please, please *don't let him think I'd actually follow his
suggestion and choose Dylan over him.*

And why hadn't he hung around to find out the truth?
Why take off and leave her behind without another word?
Just like when she'd demanded a divorce, flinging out
the words that seemed to follow her around and repeatedly punched her in the chest. Yes, she knew she'd been
the one to hurl the dog tags at him but, ultimately, it was
Mason's gorgeous back she'd been viewing when he'd left
her behind without a fight.

The memories were vivid. Back against the wall because she'd needed the support, slowly sinking to the
floor as her heart had ached so hard she thought it would
collapse under the sorrow-filled weight. And this morning, when she'd woken up and he'd been *gone,* she hadn't
wanted to admit how much that moment had reminded
her of him walking out on her all those years ago. When
he had climbed into The Beast and simply driven away.

Because he didn't discuss. He grunted and took off.

Split without a backward glance.

And the feeling was so familiar, so painful—and *this*
time, undeserved—that by the time she rounded a corner and spied the back of The Beast, Reese was fuming.

Gripping the wheel tight, Reese floored the convertible and sailed past the red truck, honking her horn and
not caring that she was acting like a crazed driver. Mason
steered off onto a dirt road that wound through a copse
of trees. Reese braked hard and made a sharp U-turn to
double back and follow his dusty trail. A maintenance access, it appeared, as Mason came to a stop next to a small

metal building that looked to house the groundskeeper's equipment. Reese pulled in behind him.

She parked behind the truck and jumped out of her car, not caring her heels sank into the sandy road. Her pulse was already pumping hard, and the difficult path only made it worse.

Reese refused to consider the irony that it was like running through quicksand.

"You almost ran me off the road," Mason said, a doubtful scowl on his face as she jerked open the passenger door. "What the hell are—"

"Where are you going?" she said.

There was a ten-second pause in which Reese was sure every autonomic function in her body shut down one by one. No heartbeat. No breathing. And now her brain seemed to be malfunctioning, too.

Until she filled in the answer for him. "You were leaving."

God, even speaking the words out loud hurt.

Mason stared at her a moment before turning off the truck. He shifted to face her, but his expression was hardly reassuring. Or welcoming. "Yes."

"I asked you to wait." Furious, she hauled herself up into The Beast, cursing the limitations her skirt put on her ability to pull the act off gracefully. She slammed the door shut. "Was that too much to ask?"

A flash of irritation crossed his face.

He'd showered before he'd made tracks for his truck, his hair damp, ruffled. The whole package extra delicious, and the memories of all they'd shared last night—what they'd shared all those years ago in this very cab—were hard to ignore when he smelled good and looked even better. His dog tags sparkled against the olive-green shirt that matched his eyes, the well-worn jeans snug across his hips. And, after last night, she was sure she'd never be able to settle for another man's arms ever again.

Which was a terrifying thought. Especially since he'd written them off before they'd even had the chance to begin anew.

When he remained silent, she tried again. "What part of *don't go anywhere* did you not understand?"

His responding grunt only infuriated her more, and the anger breached the dam and came out in a rush. She clenched her teeth, thumping her hand against his hard chest. Frustrated.

Furious.

"Quit with that stupid grunt that doesn't say anything," she said, and the sting in her hand left her shaking her fingers from the pain. "I thought you'd matured since the days you wouldn't talk to me."

"Maybe I don't know what the hell to say. The grunt is my default response," he said. "And I don't appreciate being ordered around like a friggin' private."

"If you would just act like an adult and stop avoiding the issues we might be able to work a few things out."

"We?" he said, his sharp bark of humorless laughter cutting deep. "We were never able to work anything out." His gaze relentless, he tipped his head. "And I'm *not* the only one who needed to grow up."

"Well, that's rich. You're the one who keeps running out on *me*," she said. "*You're* the one who keeps shutting down, issuing grunts instead of sentences and then pulling a disappearing act." The frustration reached astronomical levels, and all the old resentment came pouring out. "Jeez, Mason. Why do you think I wanted a divorce? After waiting forever for you to come home, and then with all the problems we were having, you barely said a word outside of civil conversation."

"You spoke enough for the two of us."

"I know I made mistakes." She barreled on despite him, the years of regret, pain and bitterness making her words hard. "But then you went and reenlisted. You chose to go back to *Afghanistan* rather than stay with your *wife*."

The force of his words matched the hand he thrust through his hair. "Why do you think I went back?"

The question stunned her, and she froze, her mind instantly recognizing she wasn't going to like the turn in the conversation.

Dreading his response, her voice balancing on a shaky edge, she said, "Because it was easier to face deployment than to have to talk to me."

"Being your husband was hard as hell," he said, and Reese's breath caught.

Her heart shrank back from the words. "I know I pushed you too hard."

"That's not what I'm talking about."

"Then what *are* you talking about?"

He turned to stare out the window of the truck, offering her a view of his profile as she waited, unable to breathe. Maybe she'd overcompensated, but she'd done everything in her power to make the marriage work, and now he was telling her she'd been the problem?

When Mason turned that hazel gaze back on her, the resignation in his eyes was profound. "Because you're an impossible woman to be married to, Reese." Her jaw almost hit the seat as he went on. "I went back because my job was always easier than being married to you."

She gaped at him. "Defusing bombs was easier than living with me?"

"Yes." He huffed out a humorless laugh. "Defusing bombs was easier than dealing with you."

She blinked, pushing back the sting of tears, trying to digest his words. Trying to understand what had been so difficult about being married to Reese Michaels.

"At least with my job I was making a difference," he said. "I was a vital part of a team. My work made me feel important." He turned his gaze back to hers. "People needed me."

"*I needed you.*"

He shot her a look that melted her to the core. "You made me feel *irrelevant*."

The *tick, tick, tick* sound of the cooling engine filled the truck, the faint smell of motor oil reaching her nostrils. Even as her heart slowly shifted higher, lodging firmly in her throat, cutting off her air.

He shook his head, the movement slight, the meaning monumental. "Your parents..." he said, his voice harsh.

And then looked as if he were searching for the right words.

For a brief moment, blessed vindication flared. Surely he was dead wrong in his assessment. And right now, she really needed him to be wrong.

She inhaled swiftly. "You are not going to blame our problems on my parents."

"It was your relationship with them that was the problem." He didn't look her in the eye. "Because you were only too happy to let them treat you like a pampered princess," he went on, her heart shrinking further. Until it was just a raisinlike version of its former self.

Leaving the blood draining from her face.

"Princess?" she croaked.

She *hated* the nickname.

"Ah, come on, Reese," he said. Clearly exasperated, he finally twisted to face her completely. One hand gripped the top of the steering wheel, the other clutched the seat behind her head. His knee flattened on the bench between them. "Every time we had a problem you ran home to Mommy and Daddy. You never turned to *me*. If something came up, it was your parents you asked for help. For input or advice. If you had a problem that needed to be solved, your parents threw money at it and—" he threw his hand in the air "—voilà, instafix."

The rapid-fire blinking of her lids didn't clear her up-close view of the anger on his face.

"That's not true," she said.

But the words came out weak, because the ten-year-old memories were coming back. Piling up one by one. The wall of blame building so high she knew she'd never be able to tear it down.

Memories of her contacting her father when the dishwasher broke. Instead of being repaired, her parents had had a top-of-the-line brand-new one installed. One that had looked glaringly out of place in their little house. And when The Beast needed new tires, instead of discussing the issue with Mason, she'd called her parents. Who had immediately sent a brand-new truck with all the latest gadgets and whistles.

She'd never been able to figure out why Mason had hated the shiny SUV on sight. She'd thought he was being ungrateful. Had called him exactly that to his face. Because she'd thought she was smoothing things over. Making life easier.

It never occurred to her that she was screwing everything up. It never occurred to her that she was cutting Mason out of the equation.

Leaving him feeling like the odd man out.

"Maybe I needed to feel like you needed me, instead of letting your family solve every issue that came along." His grip on the wheel grew tight, his knuckles white, his expression grim. And then he let out a defeated sigh. "I didn't resent your upbringing, Reese."

His gaze wasn't as angry now, shifting more to one of defeat. Which only hurt more, not less. "But I sure as hell began to resent being the poor dumb grunt who couldn't be trusted with the little decisions, much less the big ones."

"Jeez, Mason," she said, closing her eyes.

Was that just his version? Or was it the brutal truth?

And now that he'd stopped using his standard grunt as a default response, had finally told her what had been going through that mind of his, the words were more painful than she could have imagined. All this time she'd been so sure that he'd been the main reason their marriage had failed. That his alpha attitude and close-lipped ways had delivered the fatal blow to their relationship. So, clearly the fault lay mostly at *his* feet, not hers.

And she'd been too selfish to see the truth.

The discussion she'd tried to have ten years ago now left her feeling completely raw.

"I needed you," she said, closing her eyes. Devastated to learn that she'd had such a massive role in killing their happiness, she fought back the sting of angry tears. Angry at herself for being so stupid. Angry at Mason for not being able to tell her the truth until now. But mostly angry that they seemed stuck in the past, still trying to figure out how to get beyond their mistakes.

Fear. Shame. And pain. She longed to bury them all.

And when she turned to face him, his seductive scent filled her nostrils, bringing a pang of memories. Thick, crescent-shaped black lashes framed a pair of hazel eyes that blazed so bright they burned her to ashes. On impulse, she reached out and clutched his shirt, the dog tags beneath, and her fingers curled around the metal. "I needed you," she repeated.

Because, God, it was the only truth she had left.

Desperate to make her point, stirred by the feel of his hard chest, she hauled him closer. "I needed you—" meeting his gaze with a look she hoped conveyed her sincerity "—and I still do."

And then she captured his lips with hers.

The pleasure of tasting Reese again was so great Mason just managed to refrain from groaning, damning himself for being so weak. But objectivity was hard to maintain with Reese's mouth moving over his, and Mason's breath stuttered to a stop as he gripped her shoulders with the lofty thought of pushing her away. Instead, he spent several seconds enjoying her flavor, opening wider to take more.

The fleeting moment was filled with indecision. He could push her away and maintain his pride. He could give in to the remembered anger and cling to the fury. It would be the safest plan.

She tugged harder on his dog tags, urging him closer, and Mason slicked his tongue against hers, spiking his pulse dangerously high.

Between drugging, hypnotic kisses, Reese said, "Why did you drive away?"

Mason spread his hands across her back, pressing the soft curve of her breasts to his chest, and recited the words he'd been telling himself as he'd driven away. "It's time for me to leave."

Which was a ridiculous statement considering he currently had her in a hold she couldn't break, even if she wanted to.

Thing was, she didn't seem to want to.

She trailed her mouth to his neck. "I thought we were just getting started," she said with a voice that sounded wrecked, and then raked her teeth across his bounding pulse, as if to leave a mark.

Desire decked him hard, and he fisted his fingers in the fabric covering her back, torn between the need to pull her away and the need to tear off her shirt. Between the need for self-preservation and the overwhelming urge to make love to the one woman who made him feel like this was where he belonged.

Reese, who always sounded so broken in his arms. Shattered by her need for *him*.

He slaked his mouth across hers, holding her captive against his chest as he tried to resolve the war raging in his head.

"Just getting started?" He nipped her lower lip before going on, breathing the words into her open, willing mouth. "We used to screw each other's brains out during our marriage," he said, not caring he sounded so crude. "And that sure as hell didn't help anything. Did you think we would make love again and everything would be okay?"

And the words were directed as much at himself as at Reese. But, damn, the question seemed stupid. Because he felt better than okay.

He felt fantastic.

Alive.

More so in her arms than ever, especially since that damn blast had stolen a part of his life from him.

But... "Sex won't solve anything," he rasped against her mouth.

"Of course it won't."

Despite the words, he fed his need for her, his lips moving with a desperation that he should have been better at controlling. His tongue sought hers as he lost himself in the seductive, welcoming warmth of her mouth. Her hands smoothed across his shoulders and then down, tracing the wings tattooed on his back as if to heal him. Of exactly what he wasn't sure.

Time hadn't healed the problems between them. If anything, their situation was worse. Because now they had bitter proof that desire, *love,* sometimes wasn't enough. And Mason was just a fraction of his former self.

He wasn't even *whole.*

As if to remind him of exactly that, when Reese slid her skirt up and swung her leg over his lap, her thigh caught on the small, dog-eared notebook in his front pocket. The motion knocked the pad to the seat beside them, where it lay, splayed open to all the notes he'd taken that day. Lists to keep him straight. A required accessory in his life now. A necessary companion. Reminding him of just how broken he was.

Because now he couldn't keep track of his sorry life without help.

Mason frowned and loosened his grip on her shirt, but Reese misinterpreted the signal and pulled off her blouse, tossing it aside. Breasts cupped in sheer lace, she shifted closer, eyes dark as her thighs pressed around his. As her center inched closer to the bulge at his crotch, Mason thought he would die.

And, *damn*, he seemed incapable of keeping his hands off her now. He knew she'd been saying goodbye to Dylan and the scene had been torture to watch. Because part of him wanted to keep her for himself. And the other part, the brutal, realistic part, wanted her to get the happily ever after that he wasn't capable of giving her.

They were impossible on so many levels.

One night spent cleaning up after Mason—taking care of him while he was laid up and useless—did not mean the princess he'd married was ready for the harsh reality of a man with his diagnosis. No matter how subtle his injury appeared on the surface. Reese was oblivious, because Mason had yet to work up the courage to share the full extent of the consequences of his wounds.

He swallowed down the guilt and self-directed scorn.

Mason's frown grew deeper. "Tell him you made a mistake," he said, ignoring her protest even as he cupped her breasts through the delicate lingerie. She sucked in a breath and arched into his hands, making continuing more difficult. "Tell him last night was my fault—"

Her lips landed on his again, drawing him in, taking

him down, her tongue feasting on his as she unhooked her bra.

"I'm not going to lie, Mason." She tossed the scrap of lace aside. "Not to myself or anyone else."

Gripping the soft skin of her thighs, Mason pulled back to stare up at her. Her face was flushed, her golden hair disheveled, the spun sunshine mussed and tousled. Her sweet smell clouded his senses. Her lovely breasts were close enough to touch...and he *needed* to touch.

Just like he needed the oxygen in the air.

His gaze trapped in the blue of hers, she clutched the hem of his shirt and dragged it over his head.

"Look," he said, his protest coming out weaker than he would have liked. "We tried this before and failed. I think you're better off with D—"

She thumped her fist against his chest again, a frown crossing her face.

"Is it too much to ask to have someone fight for me?" she said, and he couldn't answer. Because the next thing he knew Reese was wilting against him, as if weary of the argument. She skimmed her hands down his bared chest, tracing his muscles. Her soft lips and gentle teeth nibbled at his jaw. "Just once?"

He should tell her about his injuries.

He should confess the truth.

But in her relentless pursuit of him, she kissed, licked and then bit down hard at the curve where his neck met his shoulder. Pleasure streaked straight to his groin. When he opened his mouth to come clean, her lips feathered against his skin, and the words wouldn't come out....

It was a hell of a thing to realize he was as powerless in her arms as he was in the grips of a migraine.

And then her hands dropped to his crotch and freed his erection, tracing the hard flesh that burned a hundred times brighter with her touch. Groaning, he dipped his head to her neck, inhaling the scent of crème brûlée, his throat thick with want.

She arched against him in a maneuver that left him swearing. "Mason," she said, her voice shattered.

Almost a prayer. Definitely a beg.

And there was nothing for it. For the fourth time in twenty-four hours, he was going to make love to Reese.

Awash in pleasure, aching for her, Mason finally gave himself over to the feeling as he swept aside the crotch of her panties and thrust deep, relishing the feeling of being enveloped in her sweet heat.

As he began to move beneath her, he speared his fingers in her hair, tipping her head back. His lips, teeth and tongue feasted on the creamy skin of her neck before he arched her over his arm to focus on the breasts that were the perfect size. His mouth closed around a nipple, and Reese called out. He dropped his hands to her buttocks, clutching her close as he pumped into her with all the fever and frustration of their missing years—a long, painful ten-year gap.

Their appetite for each other might not have solved their marital problems, but...*damn*...

With Reese still wrapped in his arms, he shifted on the seat of The Beast so he could bring her closer, knowing it was way too late for second thoughts.

Mason closed his lids, mesmerized by the soft, short, sharp sounds that broke from Reese's mouth with every thrust. As if she were just managing to keep it together, skirting the edges of flying apart. And every harsh gasp, her every moan wound something tighter in Mason. With each arch of his hips, the white rush of heat coursed through him, so close to completion his eyes nearly rolled back in his head.

And then Reese gripped his back, eyes wide, the noises trapped in her throat as she came.

The sheer force of her pleasure tripped the pressure plate in his groin, triggering an explosion so great, an orgasm so consuming his every cell burned. And the white light in his head flashed bright, bursting behind his lids, blinding him with its intensity.

When the world slowly righted itself and Mason settled back on Earth, his vision finally functioning again, Reese shifted against him, and his body began to assimilate sensory information. Savoring the simple sensation of holding Reese. Her sweet scent. Her warmth. Last night had been more like a fantasy. The dark and the quiet and the relative silence—outside of Reese's broken moans—contributing to the dreamlike sensation.

Now, as the sun filtered through the trees, dappling them both with light, holding her felt more real. More ripe for tension.

Where the hell did they go from here?

"We should get you back to your party preparations," he said.

Her face buried in his neck, thighs clasping his hips tight, Reese tightened her arms around his shoulders, fingers stroking his back. As if trying to trace the individual feathers on his makeshift wings.

"Don't leave, Mason," Reese murmured, the words

whispering across his skin. "At least stay through to-morrow."

He closed his eyes, hating the thought of attending the Big Event. Bad enough it was originally set to celebrate Reese's marriage to Dylan, but, with his stupid short-term memory problems, each introduction would be a nightmare. A crowd full of people he didn't know. And he couldn't realistically jot down the name of every person he met.

A surge of anxiety left him scowling in her hair, sweat dampening his neck.

"I don't think your family or friends will be too thrilled with my presence," he said.

"Having you there will make me feel better."

"You know I suck at small talk." He paused before going on. "I suck at communication period."

And he wasn't such an ass as to think that his tendency to keep his thoughts to himself hadn't factored into their marital problems.

She blinked and brushed the sweat-soaked hair from his forehead and leaned in, kissing the scar at his temple.

"It just takes work, Mason," she said.

But words hadn't been necessary when he was sprawled on the ground, concentrating on his job. Carefully brushing away dirt to expose wires made sense. Pressure plates, battery packs and detonators set to explode, *those* he understood. He was familiar with the construction. Accustomed to the design. And while the devices were deadly, there was still a formula to follow.

Out here in this world, all bets were off.

Still straddling his lap, Reese sat back a bit and looked at him. "Just be your usual charming self."

His lips twitched at her dry tone and he studied her for a moment, sweeping a stray strand of her tousled hair from her forehead. "Why is this party so important to you?"

Her kiss-roughened lips parted slightly in surprise, and she remained silent, her blue eyes wide. He could tell she was struggling to come up with the words.

"I've screwed up so much," she said.

His fingers curled at her waist, pressing into her soft skin.

"I guess..." She paused again. "I just..." Her eyes crinkled at the corners as she fought to get the words out. "I just needed for this...for this to end with me holding my head high."

Pride.

He could understand that. His ego had sustained repeated blows while married to Reese, and while he was sure that she hadn't been doing it on purpose—had been completely, naively oblivious to the effects of her actions—it stung nonetheless.

"Will you stay?" she said. "Please?"

The hitch in his chest was instinctive. A little protective twitch of anxiety on her behalf. Because, crap, those baby blues were looking at him like she was a deserted puppy and the rest of the pack was long gone. He closed his eyes, trying to shut out the vision and the certainty that the party would end disastrously for him.

With a slow exhalation, he finally lifted his lids. "Fine," he said. "I'll stay."

He was rewarded with a kiss that blew his concentration to hell, lighting a fuse that sizzled with the promise of another blast of pleasure to his body. So, with

Reese still wrapped in his arms, his mouth on her lips, he twisted until she was beneath him on the seat of The Beast.

And, despite his inevitable sense of doom about tomorrow, despite having made love to her four times in the past twenty-four hours, he threw himself into number five.

TWELVE

The back of the limo was beautiful. Plush, black leather seats. Killer sound system. And a full bar complete with beautiful crystal glasses. Too bad the mood wasn't as celebratory as the posh surroundings demanded. Reese remained silent as she stared out the window while her friends attempted to fill the silence.

"I've never attended a bachelorette party before," Cassie said.

"It's not a bachelorette party," Marnie drawled. "It's an afternoon at the spa."

"I thought we were going to enjoy a night on the town," Gina replied, sounding disappointed.

Reese knew that Marnie had been planning this outing into the city for ages. And despite coming back from her showdown with Mason feeling happy and hopeful and helplessly screwed up, positive she was going to lose her mind, Reese had gone along with Marnie's plan for the rest of the day. She didn't have the heart to tell her friends her life had changed so thoroughly—that she was mooning over her ex, *again*—because they might not be so patient and understanding the second time around.

The three women had been tiptoeing around her as if she might break. And Reese knew they were dying to ask her why she'd shot off after Mason like a dingbat out of hell. Worse, once they got started, Reese knew they would ask too many questions. Questions that she didn't have answers to.

Like...exactly how did she feel about Mason?

"I originally ordered the pampered package," Marnie said, clearly ignoring the two brunettes facing her and Reese. "Massages, manicures, pedicures. A gourmet dinner with a bird's-eye view of New York City."

"I'd settle for the Cosmo package right now." Reese heard Gina rummaging through the available liquor bottles. "Hopefully there'll be hot men at some point?" she said. "Because I definitely think there should be hot men. Especially now that we're celebrating an *un*bachelorette party."

Reese's stomach dipped—

"Technically, Reese is more of a divorcée than bachelorette," Cassie said.

And then Reese's stomach flipped—

"I told you," Marnie said, her drawl growing thicker. "It's an afternoon at the spa that ends at a fabulous restaurant, not at a male strip club."

Until Reese couldn't take the nausea anymore.

Staring at her hand on the window, she said, "He left because of me."

She pressed her fingers to the glass as her chest shut down. Refused to work. Which made breathing next to impossible. Because no matter how much time had passed, she couldn't forget the look on Mason's face when he'd finally exchanged those grunts for words.

Words that had hurt.

"I assume we're talking about the ex-husband," Gina said with a careful tone. "And not the ex-fiancé?"

Reese dug her nails into her palms, and the tires brushed the rumble strip, filling the limo with a shuddering sound. When the noise passed, she looked up and into three pairs of eyes that were staring at her with concern. The women who meant the world to her. The ones she felt safe with. The ones she'd needed ever since Dylan had called the wedding off, ever since Mason Hicks had landed back in her life. Or, more accurately, ever since Mason had left her behind to reenlist.

"He reenlisted, shipped back to Afghanistan to escape *me*." Reese sucked in a sharp breath, the air burning her lungs. "To escape his bratty *wife*."

Dressed in a classy sundress, Marnie slipped an arm around her shoulders. "You weren't a brat, Reese."

The limo continued to motor down the road. Across from Reese and Marnie, Cassie, dressed in khakis and a T-shirt with the words *Astronomy GEEK,* remained silent. Gina, attired in a sexy miniskirt and sheer blouse fit for a nightclub, sat back in her seat and said nothing, as well. But the looks on their faces and the lack of support for Marnie's statement said it all.

"I was, wasn't I?" Reese said

Flicking a fingernail across her knee, Gina evaded her gaze. "Was what?"

Reese bit back the bitter smile. "Spoiled."

Gina spared a glance for the other two women before replying. "Well...we didn't call you Park Avenue Princess just because of where you grew up."

"Why didn't you tell me I was a spoiled rotten brat?" Reese said, knowing the question was ridiculous.

"You weren't a brat," Cassie repeated soothingly, her face sincere. "You were just spoiled rotten." The looks the other two shot her had her amending her statement. "But in a good way," the Aussie hurried on.

"Seriously?" Despite everything, Reese gave a small laugh. "The word *rotten* is never attached to anything good." She tipped her head questioningly at her friends. "Did you all think I ran to my parents to solve all my problems, too?"

Again, three women shifted in their seats, looking too uncomfortable to comment. Which was all the comment she really needed. Jeez. Mason wasn't alone in his views, which meant there was no escaping the truth.

Reese planted her elbow on the backseat and dropped her head to her hand.

Cassie looked as if she was lost as to what to say next. "Are we supposed to still be mad at the ex?"

Gina let out a small bark of laughter. "Which ex?" She pulled out one of the bottles of champagne she'd snagged before they left Bellington and popped the cork. "The ex-husband or the ex-fiancé?"

"Gina," Marnie said, nodding her head toward Reese with concern on her face. "Maybe champagne isn't an appropriate drink right now."

Gina retrieved four crystal champagne flutes from the bar and began to pour. "Have you seen how many bottles there are in the kitchen back at the estate?" She handed a glass to Marnie and one to Reese. "And this is the good stuff. I think the ex-fiancé can afford to donate a few bottles toward our celebration. Given all that's happened, it's the least he can do."

Reese pressed her lids closed. "Dylan was only marrying me because he didn't mind taking care of me."

No surprise her parents had been the ones to suggest she assume the role as chairman of the fundraising committee for The Brookes Foundation. In the beginning she'd spent a lot of time with Dylan, learning the ins and outs. Interacting with the board members. Making future plans. Without Dylan, she couldn't have navigated such a huge job. But she hadn't *really* been making her own way; she'd just been trading one dependent relationship for another. Her parents for Dylan. It was a difficult concept to wrap her head around.

And she'd thought they'd made such a great team.

"But I don't want to be someone my husband doesn't *mind* spending the rest of his life with." Reese watched the bubbles in her glass, thinking of Mason. And the regret...? The regret was almost crippling. All these years of being angry at him, but she was as much, maybe *more,* to blame than him. "I want to be the one he can't live without," she finished softly.

The tires hit the rumble strip again, and the thudding vibration resonated in the limo. Which was fitting since her heart was now doing the same thing, because she'd just realized she still loved Mason. Had never *stopped* loving him.

And, dear *God,* her brain had stopped functioning.

Stunned, Reese watched Gina hand the last glass to Cassie.

But Cassie looked unconvinced. "So—" her face twisted

into an expression of doubt "—just what are we celebrating?"

Reese let out a sharp bark of laughter that bordered on manic and then composed herself, not wanting to ruin Marnie's plans for the afternoon.

"We—" Gina lifted her champagne flute and looked at each of them "—are celebrating the return of the Awesome Foursome."

Instantly a watery smile of gratitude hit Reese. The current messed-up state of affairs had consumed all of their energies, leaving no room for rehashing old resentments. They'd eventually have to address the issues. But for now, it was good to simply enjoy their company. To have her friends by her side again.

"What are you going to do next?" Gina said, her dark eyes on Reese.

She loved Mason.

What was she going to do?

"I don't know," she said.

Marnie placed a comforting hand on Reese's shoulder. "We're here for you, honey," she said. "No matter what happens."

Reese gripped her glass and blinked back the surge of emotion, feeling incredibly grateful. Because, with tomorrow's party rapidly approaching, she had a feeling she was going to need all the help she could get.

The tents looked beautiful in the setting sun, delicate swaths of royal blue draped across the ceilings and trailing gently to the deck. The tables looked lovely, the ice vases—minus the engraved names—each holding a cluster of white orchids. Simple. Elegant. And with the truffles at each place setting now housed in royal blue cellophane, and not the silver engagement ring boxes, the tables looked a little less like a wedding reception.

Spying Gina at the bar, Reese made her way to join her, feeling pleased, until she saw the paper lanterns adorning the counter.

Reese's heart sank. "Who put out the lit-up bar menus?" she groaned.

All of this time she'd been scurrying around, trying to erase all visible evidence of the celebration that was *supposed* to have taken place today. How could she have forgotten this detail?

"Beats the hell out of me," Gina said. "And what's wrong with them? They're beautiful." Gina slid the offending decoration closer to read the inscription. Each side listed out the available drinks, written in a script that was an exact replica of the wedding invitations each guest had received...with the words *Reese and Dylan* scrolled ornately across the top.

"Oh," Gina said simply. And then she pursed her lips. "What's a Nojito?"

"It's a Mojito without the alcohol."

"Sounds like a waste of perfectly good mint and lime juice," Gina said as she repositioned the lantern on the bar.

Nerves stretched taut, Reese murmured, "And I need all the alcohol I can get right now."

"This wedding-that-wasn't party *is* stressful," Gina said, and Reese shot Gina a sarcastic *you-think?* look before the woman went on. "I practically had to tackle the DJ to get his list of songs and ensure he'd cut the inappropriate ones."

Reese sent Gina a grateful smile. "I don't know what I would have done without everybody's help."

And then she spied Mason, and Reese's heart skipped enough beats to make her feel woozy, killing her smile. He was talking to Parker and Amber. Her brother and her friend had their pinkie fingers loosely linked, a subtle act of PDA that for anyone else would be unremarkable. For her brashly bullheaded, relentlessly sarcastic, hands-off older brother it was a major miracle.

He'd actually managed to give Reese a hug earlier. An awkward one, maybe, but a hug nonetheless. She had no memory of him ever doing that before, and hopefully it meant they'd moved beyond the way their mother had treated them and could now establish a relationship as adults. A fresh start as brother and sister. Like she longed for a fresh start with Mason.

And the way Amber and Parker looked at each other had Reese blinking back a conflicting surge of delight for them and nostalgia for herself. She remembered when she used to wear that same expression. That glow of utter happiness.

And love.

Reese was still adjusting to how quickly the two had flipped head over heels, and she wasn't the only one. Every relative she had was surprised by the whirlwind relationship. Evidently the ability to fall hard and fast ran in the family, the love-at-first-sight gene passed on from their mother to her brother and Reese.

Her mother's attempt had ended in failure. Parker was too stubborn to fail. And Reese...

Reese shifted her eyes to her ex. In dress pants and a long-sleeved, button-down shirt of pale blue, Mason looked fit and handsome and so beautiful that her stomach rolled in that terrifyingly visceral way that screamed "I'm in love." For all intents and purposes, she hadn't *really* let herself anywhere near the sensation since she'd hurled those dog tags at him, essentially ending their marriage. Unfortunately, it was back with a vengeance.

And much worse the second go-round.

She'd been young and stupid all those years ago, and not because she'd impulsively married Mason. No, in her perpetually clueless state, she'd ruined her only chance at happiness.

"You've got to tell him how you feel, hon," Marnie drawled from behind her.

Her eyes burning with emotion, Reese turned and took in the concerned faces of the three friends who had gathered behind her.

Gina, in her chic, sophisticated gown that hugged a figure that would make most men weep. Cassie, her beauty finally enhanced with makeup, her glossy brunette hair gently curling at the ends. Gina had loaned the stargazer a sleeveless, V-neck dress in a beautiful shade of eggplant that wrapped around her waist, emphasizing the figure Cassie couldn't be bothered to embellish. And then there was Marnie, her blond hair swept up off her neck, the graceful Southern manners always present, no matter how many years since she'd left that world behind.

Marnie's words echoed in Reese's brain: *You've got to tell him how you feel...*

She was terrified at the thought.

Petrified by the potential for failure.

But, ultimately, she knew Marnie was right.

* * *

The redheaded, wedding-gown guru Mason had met the first day looked even nicer all dolled up, and the whipped look on Parker's face was pretty comical. Clearly Reese's brother was smitten. Too bad Mason couldn't remember his girlfriend's name.

You would think his screwed-up brain could at least commit the major details to memory when it came to a pretty woman.

The three of them were about halfway through a conversation about people Mason didn't know when a relative of Parker's stole the happy couple away, and Mason blew out a breath in relief. He rolled his arms back trying to release the tension currently wrenching his shoulder blades together, and had been since the moment he'd entered the party. A social challenge of the highest order for a man whose verbal recall was crap. His visual memory was much better, but he couldn't exactly walk around writing down everyone's name in his notebook like a cop taking notes at a crime scene.

"Thanks for sticking around."

Heat snaked up his spine at the familiar female voice coming from behind. And while Reese sounded perfectly calm, the underlying sensual thrum she evoked made him long to drag her to his truck and draw out every one of the splintered moans he'd missed during the past ten years. But when Mason turned, the vision of Reese blasted coherent thought to holy hell.

The low light added a smokiness to her blue gaze that made him think of long nights, hot, sweaty sex and the soft, supple give of her mouth beneath his. Her dress was simple, peach and strapless and ended midthigh, which

had the advantage of showing off the legs that had strad-
dled him in the truck yesterday.

Mason forced back the memory and gave a small shrug.
"You asked me to stay, so I stayed." He took a moment to
check out her lovely form. "I like the dress," he said, and
then his eyes crinkled in humor as he spied the side zip-
per. "No buttons, I take it."

The slow sensual curl at the edges of her lips, he feared,
had his mouth opening and closing slightly in a sound-
less attempt to attain a sense of equilibrium in the presence of his sexy ex-wife's smile.

Who was whipped now?

Worse, the smile contained a fragment of promise or
inevitability or *something* that made it clear that Reese
no longer saw her ex-husband as someone she wanted to
go away. And it was that hint of hope he saw in her eyes
that suddenly had him scared senseless.

"Do you have my name written in your little black
book?" she said.

"My little black book?" he said, confused.

Because he was pathetic enough to still be reeling from
the effects of her smile.

But everything got worse when she stepped forward
and he was instantly bombarded by her sweet smell and
her heat and a pair of eyes that still had the power to
drown him. When she reached into his shirt pocket and
pulled out the notebook, his body was so intent on taking in every sensation that he couldn't move.

And when she waved the small pad in front of his face,
a bitter scoff escaped his mouth.

If only his little black book *was* just a crass tool for
keeping track of female acquaintances.

As he watched her dangle the notepad, a part of him wanted to grab it back. But another part of him realized that he wanted her to see. He wanted her to know exactly how much effort he put into getting through his day.

Just how screwed up his brain was.

But before she could scrutinize his shameful list, a waiter wandered by with a platter of red caviar in the shape of a heart. A striking arrangement that was now making its way around the room, several waiters weaving through the crowd with the exact same display as they served the crowd. Reminding each guest that, at one point, this party had been originally planned to celebrate a wedding. Nuptial bliss. *Commitment.*

The shocked look on Reese's face as she took in the appetizer cut off whatever she'd been about to say. Notebook clutched in her fingers, she dropped her hand to her side, staring as a second server wandered by with another bright red heart.

Mason had to admit the platters were kind of pretty, if you were into that kind of thing.

He hiked an eyebrow at Reese, who currently looked as if her lungs were being pulled from her chest. "I hate caviar," he said dryly. "But, if you want, I can take a spoon and smear a big crack in each one as the waiters go by."

There was a stunned second where Reese just stared at him, her lids slowly opening and closing as if in a trance.

And then she started giggling, low at first, but persistent. As the seconds ticked by, the sound slowly grew in intensity. Until she had to sit in a chair and hold her stomach to keep the noise from escaping from her mouth *too* loudly. As she fought to subdue the laugh, her shoulders shook with the effort.

Mason shot her a wary look, worried she was finally cracking under the pressure. "Are you okay?"

"It's just..." she said, still battling a serious case of the giggles. "The stress of the last few days..."

He waited for her to go on.

"Dylan..." she said.

Reese wiped a tear of amusement from the corner of her eye. "Your return..."

The words hit him particularly hard. She seemed incapable of finishing a sentence as she swiped at a wet track on her cheek and slowly shook her head, her mouth twisting with humor. "Trying so hard to remove every trace of the wedding from this party."

He wasn't sure if she was going to explode in a good way...or bad.

"Are you sure you're okay?" he said.

"I'm positive."

She gazed up at Mason, and he was struck by the look in her eyes. The clarity. The resolve. She *was* okay, which was surprising considering all she'd been through. That she'd finally found the humor in the situation was nothing short of amazing. But nothing could have prepared him for what she said next.

"I love you," she said.

All of Mason's nerve endings detonated simultaneously, melting his every synapse, and the shock wave that followed was paralyzing. Much like the day he'd almost been killed. He didn't know what to do with what she was handing him.

Her heart on a platter.

"Reese," he said, doubt firmly etched in his brow as

he ignored the blood throbbing in his veins. "It's been a really rough week for you."

"True," she said simply. "But I know how I feel."

He scowled, hating the way his stomach felt as if he was doing a slow-motion barrel roll. "Too much has happened," he went on, his brain scrambling for solid ground. "You're just confused—"

"No." She stood and walked toward him, splaying her hand against his chest. "Everything is now very, very clear."

As she stared up at him, Mason felt his breathing become labored, each heartbeat like a burst of automatic gunfire from inside his chest.

"I can't—" His body seemed to shut down, system by system, his throat closing over as he turned to look across the crowd at all the fully functional people going about their fully functional lives. Damn, the words were so inadequate.

He briefly closed his eyes. He couldn't put the truth off any longer.

"I'm not right, Reese," he said, hating he had to speak the words out loud.

"What are you talking about?"

Several seconds slid by, and then he slipped the notebook from Reese's hand, flipped it open and handed it back to her. It seemed the most efficient way of sharing the news. She shot him a puzzled look, as if she was trying to figure out how a little black book could have anything to do with him being "not right."

He clenched his jaw and watched her slowly turn through the pages, her face growing more and more confused. Each day was meticulously labeled and filled with notes, his entries carefully recorded. Lists of things he needed to do. Reminders about appointments. A log of the people he'd met, each clearly labeled with their name and relationship.

"I don't understand," she said, a blank look on her face.

Mason blew out a breath. "The blast didn't just leave me with headaches," he said. His stomach felt as if he'd swallowed a fifty-pound weight. "I can't remember things like I used to anymore. That's why I write everything down."

She didn't appear to be any closer to grasping what he was saying, and the feeling of inadequacy swelled to monumental proportions.

"That's why I'm so goddamn careful with my stuff, Reese. Not because I'm a neat freak or obsessive-compulsive, but because..."

He let out a humorless laugh, searching for an apt description.

"Because I've got holes that can't be repaired," he finally went on.

She stared at him a moment more, and he felt compelled to finish telling the truth. No matter how much he wanted her, no matter how much being with Reese felt right, she deserved better.

"Look," he said in a low voice, taking a step forward. Ignoring the feeling of contentment being close to her brought. "You had no idea how right you were that first day. You don't want to get sucked up into my pathology again."

His rib muscles seemed to catch, and drawing in another breath felt impossible as he waited for her response. Afraid she'd turn him away.

Afraid she *wouldn't.*

But ultimately, her reaction didn't matter. Because he realized his words that first day, when she'd looked so lovely and so livid, were the most accurate.

"Be happy, Reese."

And with that, he turned on his heel and left.

Reese watched Mason's back until he was swallowed up by a wall of people, an awful feeling of déjà vu stealing through her veins.

Until Marnie drawled in a low voice from behind. "Where did Mason go?"

Staring at where the man she loved had disappeared into the crowd, Reese fought to keep from collapsing into the pit that had opened beneath her, her stomach drawn so tight it was a wonder she was able to stand up straight. Overwhelmed by the desire to curl up into a fetal position and give in to the defeat. The sorrow. The same feeling she'd had the day Mason had turned his back on her and walked out the door.

But she wasn't that same immature girl anymore.

She was learning to stand on her own two feet. A little late, maybe. But better now than never. And nothing that she'd been through compared to what Mason had had to endure. He'd fought hard and recovered from an explosion that had nearly killed him.

Every day he got out of bed not knowing when his next crippling migraine would strike. Every night when insomnia set in, instead of complaining he simply paced the halls, patiently waiting for sleep to come. And when the explosion left him struggling with his memory, he developed a plan to compensate. He was attempting communication now, too—some of the tight-lipped grunts replaced with actual words.

Of course, he'd said things she hadn't really wanted to hear. But they needed to be said, regardless.

"Reese." Marnie's voice was full of concern. "Where did Mason—"

"He left," Reese said, cringing at the finality of the words. All those years ago she'd let him walk out of her life, too proud to go after him. "But I'm not giving up on us this time."

Mind racing as she worked on a plan, Reese faced the three women who stared at her anxiously, and then she took in the elegantly dressed throng of people filling the tents, family and friends and associates of the Brookes Foundation. And she tried to care that she was about to abandon her guests like a complete flake. No doubt they'd all think it was totally expected, just poor little Reese finally breaking down. Beating a hasty retreat. Just like everyone thought she would.

But ultimately, Mason was more important than her pride.

She turned to her old college roommates. "Will you guys take over for me here?"

Gina's eyebrows reached for the roof. "How are we supposed to do that?"

"Just make sure no one gets into a fight," Reese said with a smile.

Gina choked on her drink, but Reese bolted before her friend could go on.

The length of her stride limited by the skirt of her cocktail dress, she half jogged, half ran toward the house and her bedroom and her car keys. Each step was so painful in her high heels she finally pulled off her shoes and tossed them aside, not caring where they skittered to a halt in the massive foyer.

Every pounding heartbeat was excruciating as, barefoot, she dashed up the stairs, retrieved her purse and made her way out to her car. After turning the key in the ignition, she stomped on the gas pedal, maneuvering around the line of parked cars and peeling up the driveway. Leaving the twinkling lights of the tents behind.

Please, please, don't let Mason drive as fast as he usually does.

She gripped the steering wheel and pressed the accelerator, the twilight-backed woods racing by at a hair-raising speed. When Reese rounded a bend in the road, she saw taillights, and almost wept with relief. She pressed the gas pedal to the floor, and surged forward with a speed that was reckless.

Only to realize the truck was idling on the side of the road. She shot past The Beast before she had time to adjust her speed.

Why had he pulled off?

Had he developed another headache?

For the second time in as many days, Reese braked hard and pulled a Uie, coming to a stop on the opposite side of the road from the truck and hopping out of her car. She didn't even bother to shut the door, ignoring the rocky pavement beneath her bare feet.

"Mason," she called as she approached the driver's side window, careful to keep her voice low. "Are you getting another headache?"

"No," Mason said.

He turned those gorgeous hazel eyes on her. Seeing no

evidence of pain in his expression, Reese relaxed a fraction. Seconds passed by as she studied him, wondering how to convince him she'd changed.

That she was mature enough to handle whatever life decided to throw at them next.

She bit her lip, curling her toes against the warm pavement. "May I climb inside?"

His fingers tightened on the wheel, but she took his silence as a good sign and rounded the cab. She was even more reassured when Mason leaned over to push open the passenger door to let her in. But when she lifted her leg to climb up, her dress hindered her efforts.

"If you don't want to get a new truck," she said, trying to keep things light despite the horrendous pounding in her chest, "will you at least buy smaller tires so I don't need a ladder to climb inside?"

He huffed out a small snort of laughter, but his demeanor didn't change. He still looked as if he couldn't decide if he was glad she was here or not.

Finally hauling herself up, she closed the door and twisted to face him. "I thought you'd pulled over because you were getting another headache."

He let out his signature grunt, but this time it was followed with words.

"No," he said. "Fortunately, at this moment and time I'm pain-free." He looked at her seriously. "But I don't know how long that will last."

She studied him for a moment, and his gaze spoke volumes. The future yawned in front of them, unclear. She knew next to nothing about head injuries and had no idea what to expect. More of the same? Would he get better? Was there a possibility he could get worse? But what bothered her the most was that she wasn't even sure if he still loved her.

Her heart lurched at the thought.

"Why did you pull off the road?" she asked.

Mason blew out a breath and turned to stare out the front windshield, darkness finally descending, a full moon edging over the horizon.

"I've been sitting here trying to convince myself to do the right thing," he said slowly, as if the words were painful. "To keep driving and leave you to...to get on with your life."

Her stomach fluttered at the news. Because if Mason had stopped, that meant he didn't *want* to leave...didn't it?

"But I don't know if I'll get better or if this is as good as it gets," he said with a wave at his head. And then his voice lowered an octave. "I've just been taking it one day at a time since I left the Marines, concentrating on getting better. But I don't know what's coming next, Reese."

She gripped his shirt, and the dog tags beneath, clinging for all she was worth.

"I don't care what comes next, Mason," she said, feeling the truth of her words to the very marrow of her bones.

"I really don't care," she said. "As long as we face it together."

His lips bunched as if he was fighting the urge to give in, the hesitation in his eyes an almost palpable thing. Several breaths passed between them as time seemed to stumble to a halt, her life teetering on the precipice of possibility.

"When we tried the first time, we had everything going for us," he said. "And we still screwed it up." His eyes crinkled at the corners, as if the memory was painful. "And now..."

"And now we know how much we have to lose," she said.

She held his gaze, refusing to give in. When he shifted his gaze back to the window, she went on.

"Mason," she said, her voice ringing loud and true. "All I know is that I'd rather face uncertainty with you than all the certainty in the world with someone else."

He turned back to look at her. "Reese," he said, his voice heavy as he stabbed his fingers through his hair in frustration. "You should—"

With her free hand she placed her fingers on his lips.

"Mason," she said, looking at the man who owned her heart. "Do you love me?"

The pause wasn't long but it felt like forever, the rapid-fire flickering of his eyelashes a testament to his inner turmoil.

"From the very first day," he finally answered, and Reese blinked back the stinging prick of tears and shifted closer, inhaling his delicious scent.

"From the very first second," he went on.

She spread her hand flat against his chest. "Then that's all we need."

Breath heaving lightly, Mason studied her until she was sure he was going to turn her away, *despite* his confession. So it was a shock when Mason lifted the dog tags over his head.

"What are you doing?" she asked.

"Giving these back," he said, settling the chain around her neck.

The faint jingling sound was the most beautiful sound Reese had ever heard.

Eyes burning, she didn't dare breathe as his fingers lingered on the bare skin of her throat, his thumb gently tracing the bounding pulse in her neck.

Feeling happy and hopeful and honored to call Mason hers, the words came out clumsy and winded. "Do I get to keep them now?"

"Yeah." His face so beautiful it made Reese's heart hurt to look at him. "Turns out," he said, "I was just keeping them safe for you."

With an embarrassingly watery sniff, she wiped a hand across her eyes to clear her vision. Once she could see better, she pilfered the notebook and pencil from his pocket.

"What are you going to do with that?" Mason said.

Reese placed the pad against his chest and began to write, penciling in the same phrase at the top of every page. "I'm filling in 'make love to Reese' at the start of each day."

After a two-second pause, Mason let out a soft huff.

Fingers clutching the chain around her neck, he hauled her in until his mouth covered hers. Several delicious seconds passed before Reese was forced to come up for air, Mason's lips—delightfully warm and wet and wonderfully ruddy from Reese's kisses—curled at the edges into a huge grin.

"Trust me when I tell you," he said. "That's one thing I won't ever forget."

* * * * *

REQUEST YOUR FREE BOOKS!
2 FREE NOVELS PLUS 2 FREE GIFTS!

HARLEQUIN® KISS™

Amy Andrews brings you the next story in
THE WEDDING SEASON miniseries with

GIRL LEAST LIKELY TO MARRY

She'd never been kissed like this.

She'd never *kissed* like this.

And still she was full of him. Her head buzzed with the essence of him. Her mouth was on fire. Her belly was tight. The heat between her legs tingled and burned.

Tuck barely managed to hold on to her as Cassie kissed him as if she were an evil genius intent on wicked things and he was her latest experiment.

He pushed her hard against the door, wanting to get closer, to kiss her more deeply. But he'd forgotten it was already slightly open and she stumbled backward, their mouths tearing apart.

He grabbed for her, found her elbow, then dropped it once she'd stabilized. And then they stood staring at each other, breathing hard, not moving for a moment, neither sure which way to jump.

Tuck knew enough about women to know that look in Cassie's eyes. He knew he could pick her up, stride into her room and lay her on the bed and she'd follow wherever he took her. And enjoy every single second of it.

But he saw a whole bunch of other stuff in her eyes, too.

HKEXP20724

Most of it he couldn't decipher. But he could see her confusion quite clearly. Obviously the kiss just did not compute for Cassie.

She looked as if she needed some time to wrap her head around it. He sure did!

"Are you okay?"

Cassie nodded automatically, but she doubted she'd ever be okay again. She felt as if she'd just had a lobotomy. Could a kiss render you stupid?

"I think I should go now. Unless…" He dropped his gaze to her swollen mouth.

Cassie shook her head and took a step back. *No unless. Go, yes, just go.* He'd turned her into a dunce.

Tuck smiled at her dazed look. It was nice to have left an impression on Little-Miss-Know-It-All. "Good night, Cassiopeia."

Cassie was incapable of answering him. She feared she'd been struck mute. As well as dumb. She watched him swagger to his room opposite, slot his key in, open his door. He turned as he stepped into his room.

"I'll be right over here. If you need a cup of *shhu-gar.*"

Cassie had no pithy comeback as his door clicked quietly shut.

**Pick up GIRL LEAST LIKELY TO MARRY
by Amy Andrews, on sale July 23
wherever Harlequin books are sold.**

The stakes are high, but the prize is worth it!

AVAILABLE JULY 23!

ALL BETS ARE ON
by Charlotte Phillips

Ask Alice Ford to shine in the boardroom and it's a done deal. Ask her to go on a first date, however, and she's a quivering mess! So when she discovers that she's the target of an office bet...to get her into bed—it's her professional nightmare!

Office legend Harry Stephens is her unlikely savior. He even volunteers to teach her just how to avoid a heartbreaker. After all, it takes one to know one....

But what is Harry really after? And when his kisses throw a curveball into the situation, is Alice ready to gamble everything for love?

Dell Bestsellers

ROBERT LITTELL

The Amateur

"One of the best. A thoroughly professional and surprised-filled work."—*Los Angeles Times*

"Taut, chilling plot and a protagonist as memorable as one of Len Deighton's or Le Carre's George Smiley." —*The New York Times Book Review*

When terrorists murdered his fiancée, Charlie Heller decided to penetrate the Iron Curtain with the intent to kill. But in a world of professional killers, his chances of success were one in a million.

A DELL BOOK $3.25   #10119-0
